YOU REAP WHAT YOU SOW!

Book 1 of 'A very bad year in Mortal Dean' trilogy

Reed Lovac

You Reap What You Sow

Author: Nat Coverdale

Copyright © Nat Coverdale (2022)

The right of Nat Coverdale to be identified as author of this work has been asserted by the author in accordance with section 77 and 78 of the Copyright, Designs and Patents Act 1988.

First Published in 2022

ISBN 978-1-915492-18-0 (Paperback)
978-1-915492-19-7 (E-Book)

Book Cover Design and Layout by:
White Magic Studios
www.whitemagicstudios.co.uk

Published by:
Maple Publishers
1 Brunel Way,
Slough,
SL1 1FQ, UK
www.maplepublishers.com

A CIP catalogue record for this title is available from the British Library.

Index

New synopsis

Twenty years ago in the quiet village of Mortal Dean, Gerard Swales left school having been subjected to a series of intolerable bullying by other school pupils, sometimes bordering on torture. On the anniversary of his disappearance, a sequence of unexplained deaths occur.

Baffled and exhausted, Detective Steve Speed and his colleagues from the local Police Station, struggle to find the link between the killings, these deaths prove to be virtually unsolvable, as a serial killer prowls the area.

This is the story about strange events, what happened to these people and the consequences of their actions, prior to these attacks. Basically "you reap what you sow".

This novel is the first installment of the "A very bad year in Mortal Dean" Trilogy. Luck, either good or bad, always seems to come in threes.

Prelude: Whatsoever a man soweth, that shall he also reap. (The Holy Bible).

Chapter 1

Calm before the storm

Sergeant Paul Collison came into Mortal Dean police station staff room, and his two colleagues noted the expression on his face. It was one of preoccupation, as if something had spooked him.

"I counted the blackbirds on the telephone wire when I was driving in this evening, thirteen of them. I hate the number thirteen, always brings in bad luck when I notice it." He remarked.

"Is that what's bothering you Paul? You shouldn't get too uptight about your bloody superstitions," said Steve Speed, the old tubby detective constable.

"Never done me any wrong, Sarge," replied Simon Hixson, the young constable making coffee for his two colleagues at the start of their shift.

"Yeah; thirteen birds on a telephone wire, what's that all about? Don't mean much to me either, your heads wrecked," Steve added.

"I'm telling you, something bad will happen now," Paul replied, "Thirteen black birds should always be taken seriously."

"You should listen to him Steve, my Grace says things like that all the time, and she's always spot on," said Simon, backing up his Sergeant.

"You're like a pair of old witches; you'll be locking up black cats next."

"Listen I know you have no religion to speak of Steve, but my superstitions are all I have right now," Paul argued back.

He finished his sentence, met with disdain from Steve, who screwed his face up into a sort of grimace.

"This is a normal village with normal people, nothing ever happens here. If it does, I'll give you fifty quid."

"Okay, fifty quid, you're on mate."

Betty and Caitlin Jones were in the lounge of their mother's flat, at one of the five high-rise blocks that made up the Carmellen Estate, considered to be the rough part of the village. They were almost ready to go out to the Tug Boat Inn, the nearest pub. Betty drank from a chilled bottle of WKD whilst standing at the lounge door; she was looking in at Caitlin. The women are thirty-six year old identical twins, so when Betty was looking at Caitlin, she was really seeing herself without having to look in the mirror, they dressed differently, to declare their independent personalities, they are slim with wavy brown hair, fairly tall and their faces don't have a single blemish.

"You look fantastic tonight Sis," said Betty, Caitlin turned to face her as she drained the last drop of drink from her bottle.

"I look fabulous you mean."

"Oh! Come on let's go then," ordered Betty. Just as they were leaving an envelope plopped onto the mat from the letterbox, Caitlin bent to pick it up and opened it as Betty joined her at the front door. It was an invitation on pretty notepaper, to a party:

YOU ARE INVITED TO THE BARN, FOR A PARTY, TO CELEBRATE THE ENGAGEMENT OF RICHARD JOINER AND CATHY FRENCH. BE THERE AT 7:30PM ON SATURDAY 13 AUGUST.

The Barn is a lavish nightclub stroke community centre; it was converted ten years ago and used by the locals for functions, such as wedding receptions and village meetings. It is set out in three parts; downstairs consists of two rooms, a bar and a conference room. Upstairs is a nightclub, with two bars running either side, and in the middle is the dance floor, the seating arrangements circled around it. Before it was converted, it was just an ordinary old hay barn and the kids used to use it for games and illicit gatherings. The date of the party is only two days away.

"Oh good, we haven't been to a party for months," said Betty.

Caitlin supported her sister by saying: "Yeah; it's been a few years since we've seen either of them, in fact it's not since Richard got posted, it'll be good to catch up."

"Come on, I'm thirsty" said Betty. Stuffing the invite into her handbag, they both walked to the pub. The twins were walking arm in arm, suddenly Betty started giggling. Caitlin was bemused.

"What?"

"I remember The Barn that the party's at. Do you remember; twenty-two years ago, when we took Outlaw there?" Betty replied...

(flashback)

Outlaw, was the nickname they gave to Gerard Swales during his school days, taken from 'The Outlaw Josey Wales', a Clint Eastwood film. Gerard got a lot of bullying because he was so reclusive and timid. He was tall and skinny, had red hair and hazel eyes, his skin was pale and scaly, he would never go out in the sun or daylight, except for when he had school to go to. He lived at Brown Gale, a farm on the east side of Mortal Dean and was regularly beaten by George, his father, who didn't quite believe that Gerard was his son as he was so different from his younger siblings, Gregg and Georgina. No one liked Gerard very much and two boys in his class at the time, dared Betty and Caitlin, the most popular girls in the school, to do something to Outlaw, which he couldn't forget. Because they fancied the boys so much, they agreed.

That night they sent an invitation to Gerard's home anonymously, asking him to a party at The Barn. He went, because he was curious about who sent the invite. When he'd got there the big double door was left ajar, there wasn't any sound coming from inside, the lights weren't on. As he walked in a couple of feet, the door was slammed behind him and a lantern was lit.

"Hello Outlaw," a female voice said.

Then from behind him another person grabbed him, holding him in a bear hug. As he tried to struggle, the bear hug got tighter, and he couldn't breathe properly. Eventually he fell to his knees, as he did so another person placed a rope under his armpits and tightened a slipknot at the back. Overwhelmed by it all he passed out. When Gerard came around he was aware of hanging in the air, by the same rope he'd been tied with.

"Hey Outlaw, bet you like hanging around in places like this?" said Betty. Gerard shook his head, he didn't speak very much, his father beat into him, that he should only say something if it was very important to do so.

"Take his clothes off, let's see if he has anything impressive to show us," suggested Caitlin. They both tore off his shirt, trousers and pants. He was hanging naked in front of them.

"Big boy?" sighed Betty. "Let's tie a firework to it, see if it gets even bigger," she added. Caitlin took out a small skyrocket from the bag she was carrying, and some twine. Betty grabbed it from Caitlin.

"Make it a bit harder for me Sis," she ordered. Caitlin stroked Gerard's penis, she rubbed her thumb over his helmet, and it started to swell a bit, Gerard hadn't felt this before, and she held it up so that Betty could tie the twine around it, Gerard was helplessly dangling. He winced as Betty knotted it very maliciously and tightly.

"We don't want it to come off, do we?" She laughed, walking over for the firework, while Caitlin continued to rub Gerard, circling the head with her finger tips, all the time smiling at him, as Betty tied the skyrocket to the twine, right next to Gerard's penis.

"Right leave him! Light the firework now and get ready to run," Betty said to Caitlin.

Caitlin lit the fuse and ran to the door, the rocket started to sizzle and spark, burning along the fuse and some of Gerard's pubic hair as it burnt upwards. Betty and Caitlin had bolted the door shut and they'd gone. The rocket sparked up more and more, as Gerard started to swing and struggle to get loose, the rocket's fire was burning more pubic hair, and it was getting to the point where it would shoot off. The sparks burnt his thighs, and then a loud whistle soared from the rocket as the twine pulled tightly on Gerard's penis, the burning was unbearable and he screamed out loudly, the rocket exploded into many pieces and then it went quiet. Gerard swung helplessly, howling in pain. The laughter coming from outside was beginning to die down, suddenly the rope was cut and Gerard dropped down, onto the soft hay beneath him. Gerard's genitalia had been badly burnt and scarred, from it all. That night Gerard staggered home, albeit painfully, he had to tell his mother and father he had an accident with some candles, which is why his lap was so badly burnt, if he had told his father the real reason, he would have beaten Gerard, for being weak and not fighting back...

(back to present)

"Oh! Yeah, of course I remember," said Caitlin as they laughed in unison, and then carried on skipping to the pub, eager to enjoy their night out, and disappeared into the busy bar.

Two days later, it was Saturday evening; Betty and Caitlin were prettying themselves up for the party.

"I'm looking forward to this," said Caitlin.

"Me too, it's about time they got hitched and seeing Cathy with her sparkler on will make her head swell," replied Betty. "Can I wear your blue top?"

"Yeah, I'm wearing my black sparkly all in one tonight," replied Caitlin.

They finished dressing and got ready, left the house and made their way to The Barn. They took their usual route, walking from their parents flat down the main road to the pub, stopped off there for a couple of drinks, half an hour later they continued to the party. When they got there, quiet music was playing from the back of the building; they went inside and called out together.

"Hello, we're here, anyone coming to see to us?"

As they said that, the door slammed shut, the lights flicked from broad bright light to a dull red. They were frightened, but thinking some of their friends were playing tricks on them, they continued to look about The Barn. They walked up to the next level, Betty stood still when she got there, but Caitlin continued walking forward.

"Careful!" Warned Betty, Caitlin's foot kicked a peg stuck to the floor tied to a rope, which went to the ceiling, the peg fell over and the rope released, the hatch slammed down tightly.

They were stuck upstairs with no way out, they needed the ring pull to raise the hatch again and because the club was sound proofed, nobody would hear them calling for help. The ambient light switched over to blue, making the air feel very cold, the girls shivered and stared ahead. On the far side of the room was a figure; it was wearing a long black shiny coat, with the hood up. The hood covered the face and the coats length went all the way down to the ground. When the figure moved, it appeared to be gliding across the floor, without making a single sound. The girls are now very worried.

"Who are you, and what do you want with us?" Caitlin shouted.

The figure put its finger to its face, motioning for her to be quiet, and then moved to the left of the room, as it did so, the room went pitch black, they screamed out loud. Suddenly there was a hiss of gas, wafting towards their faces. They immediately felt drowsy and within fifteen seconds fell unconscious. When the twins awoke, their mouths felt dry and fuzzy; they looked about in their haze to see the room was lit brightly, and this hurt their eyes a little. They were both hanging, tied together from the long beam off the ceiling. Underneath them were stacks off hay bales; just like it was all those years ago, and all around the room were fireworks of various sorts and sizes. On one wall hung a piece of black card, on it were large white letters saying, **YOU CAN KEEP YOUR CLOTHES ON FOR THIS**. Caitlin looked over to the door and saw the figure standing by the hatch.

"I can smell petrol, is it petrol?" She screamed.

The figured nodded slowly and straight away, brought a lighter from the coat pocket, lit the flame, pressed it to the fuse of the first firework, it sparked into life and as that one started to go off, so did another. The figure took out the hatch ring pull from another pocket and slowly disappeared down, closing the door behind it. The girls shook and struggled as they tried to get loose, as they did that, one of the lit rockets whistled over and hit a hay bale which set it alight. The noise from the fire was frightening; it was whistling and crackling away. They screamed when the fire roared up underneath them, the smoke was starting to thicken. Flames jumped up at Betty's dress and started to burn at the bottom, she screeched as it burnt her legs, she could do nothing about it as the fire carried on up. The fire then leaped round to Caitlin, as she began kicking, the flames started burning on her stockings, they burnt away quickly and scorched her bare legs, it caught her skirt alight, this burnt off quickly too and continued up her dress, it all happened very fast and she was totally naked, she screamed as the fire burnt some of her hair. They started panicking and wriggled in the air, but because of that the fire caught hold of them even more. The twins were coughing and spluttering, from the fumes of the smoke. As the fire got more intense, loads more fireworks lit and flew, they sparked all over the place in every direction. The fire around the twins was fierce, the pains from their burns were getting unbearable, and they were squealing and crying. Betty's clothes began clinging and melting into her skin; and Caitlin's legs were searing. The fire was getting more ferocious and the fireworks were fizzing all about the room, making a very loud noise. They were setting light to everything they landed on, thanks to the petrol. The girls knew soon, they would be unconscious and stopped struggling. The fire carried on its relentless rebellion, and was burning uncontrollably. The heat had built up so much, some windows exploded outwards; the air from outside just fanned the fire even more. Some of the bottles of liquor had smashed and caught alight, they set fire to the bar. Intense flames licked up and all around. The fire had completely engulfed the barn and was well on the way to destroying it, the smoke was thick, choking and toxic. The Barn was totally aflame, wooden joists fell down, damaging floors as they did so. More windows were breaking and the fire began to rage even faster, the whole building was starting to collapse as beams and pillars were burning, a large part of the ceiling had landed on the girls, but they were already laying still. Nothing was left to salvage. After a few more hours the fire had died down to cinders. Betty and Caitlin Jones were dead.

Chapter 2

Who could have done this?

The Fire Service continued to dampen down the smoking remains of The Barn, when a shout came from one of the crew.

"Chief, there's two bodies here!"

The Chief walked to where the shouting came from. True enough there they were, two charred bodies; one partially clothed and the other completely bare, they were strangely lying with their heads together, their bodies were pointing away from each other, one facing left and the other right.

"You'd better call it in at the police station, this looks like murder, call the Inspector too he'll have to establish the cause of fire, I can smell petrol, so tell him that," he ordered. The officer who had called him over reached for his mobile phone, and proceeded to call the police. The call came into Paul Collision's extension, he picked up the phone.

"Mortal Dean Police, Sergeant Collison speaking."

"Sarge, we have a situation down here at The Barn."

"Okay Roger, keep calm; explain the details?"

"There's been a fire, the club is completely destroyed, we've found two bodies inside, you need to come and see this."

"Right, I'll call DC Speed at his house and I'll get hold of Shabby too, don't touch anything at the scene; and don't let anyone into the area, wait there until we arrive." Collison put down his phone and shouted to Simon.

"There's hell to pay down at The Barn, arson, bodies, the lot. Give Shabby a call and get him over there will you?"

"I will, right away Sarge."

Paul then called Steve Speed at his home.

"This had better be good Paul!"

"Steve, that bad luck I was talking about the other night, well it's happening. You owe me fifty quid mate!"

"What have we got Paul? Lay it down."

"Two bodies at The Barn, a fire has gutted the place; it looks suspect to the Fire Brigade."

"That is strange, because Sheila Jones called me earlier this morning. Her twin daughters didn't come home last night, like they usually do after a night out," Steve said.

Paul thought for a second.

"Could it be them?"

"They were popular girls, can't see anybody wanting to hurt them, but we'll check it out anyway. I'll be there in five minutes." Steve put down the phone and then called to his wife.

"I'm going to be a while on this one love." Brenda had just finished a night shift and gave a tired answer.

"Okay!" Steve left the house, checked round his car and got in, started it up and sped off to The Barn.

The call came through to Jack "Shabby" Stores' forensic lab. Shabby is a middle aged dapper man, always impeccably dressed and a meticulous dogged worker, Forensic Science is his field of expertise, but he also practices Pathology. Using his resources is the reason most crimes are solved in The City.

"Stores!"

"Shabby, we need you in Mortal Dean at The Barn, it's been burnt down, and there are bodies at the scene."

"Right, I'm on my way, could you call the Coroner?"

He climbed into his all in one plastic jump suit, grabbed for his case and left his office. He spoke to his assistant Sara Weaver, on his mobile phone, preparing her for the arrival of two bodies. When Shabby arrived at the scene, he was pleased that Steve had already taped up a cordon; he had also put a tent around the bodies. The Fire Inspector was starting to check over the burnt remains of the building and the local villagers were gathering to stare at the activity going on.

"Hi, Steve, fine mess you've got here, we'll need some uniform around here to keep these ghouls away and take statements," suggested Shabby.

"Call a couple of uniform in, could you?" Steve was on his mobile phone to Simon, back at the station.

"Of course, right away Steve."

Shabby walked over to the Fire Inspector first.

"Arson, then?"

"Yes, petrol was the catalyst and by the looks of it, some fireworks were the cause." The Inspector pointed out some spent nosecones of rockets.

"Fireworks don't just light on their own though do they? This was deliberate and calculated."

Shabby left the Inspector and walked over to the tent; opened the flaps and found Steve bent down over the bodies.

"I hate the smell of burnt bodies," Steve began.

"Found anything so that we can identify them?"

Steve shook his head.

"Only that Mrs Jones called me early this morning, saying that her twin daughters didn't come back home last night and now we've got two dead burnt bodies." Steve puffed his cheeks out; he was reeling from the smell.

"We'll get them back to the lab, run some dental checks. Do a thorough report. When we've done that the Coroner's post mortem will establish, what killed them. What we need to do is establish who'd do such a despicable thing and why?" Shabby continued to examine the scene.

Ten minutes later the Coroner's car squealed to a halt outside, the noise from the brakes caused the two men to put their fingers in their ears. They left the tent so that the bodies could be lifted.

"How is it that nobody heard any screams or shouts for help? The only report from the fire crew was that The Barn was burning out of control; and lurching too near to the church behind."

"Sound proofing, Steve; the top part was a discothèque, so to drown out the noise, the builders decked the place out in Styrofoam clad walls. All the locals loved it because the kids could have fun in there, and the residents nearby weren't disturbed," Shabby concluded.

"Shit! Jack, without that sound proofing, the victims trapped inside could have been heard and maybe saved," Steve shrugged and walked away; he watched the Coroner's wagon moving away up the road, with the bodies inside.

"I'm going to stay and see if I can glean some evidence from this disaster." Shabby patted Steve on the shoulder and left him to it.

"I have to visit the Jones' and tell them their daughters may be dead."

"Once we know they're identity, I will tell you straight away." Shabby continued to walk back to the middle of the scene, reconnecting with the Fire Inspector.

Steve got into his car and drove to the Carmellen Estate where the Jones' lived. There were groups of kids milling around when he arrived at the estate, they were all pulling faces and play fighting with each other. Steve stepped out of his Mercedes; met with coos from the kids, who had stopped fighting to watch him.

"Hey! Probably won't want to leave that car there?" One of the boys shouted over, and Steve flashed his warrant card.

"One scratch on this car, and I'm calling the station."

The gang of kids stayed quiet, they noticed the seriousness in his voice. He continued to walk up to the Jones' flat. He called the passenger lift and got in; but he couldn't stand the smell of urine, which met his nostrils while he rode it. He took out his handkerchief to cover his nose, the lift came to a stop on the seventh floor and Steve got out. He prepared himself for the news he had to give; he paused for a few moments. As he walked to door 708, Steve turned to look out of the windows; he could see the ruined remains of The Barn. He leaned on the stair rail and rang the doorbell. Sheila Jones answered the door, she was as pretty to look at as her daughters, and it was clear from this where they got their looks. She was very classy with her dress sense, her hair was brown and wavy, the same as Betty and Caitlin's. Sheila had the twins when she was seventeen, and she still looked fabulous at fifty-three. Sheila went to the same school as Steve, back in the City. When she met her husband Jim, they moved to Mortal Dean. They thought it would be a perfect place to live and raise a family.

"Detective Speed, you surprised me."

"Have the girls come home yet Mrs Jones?"

"No, I'm really worried now."

"Did you know there was a fire at The Barn last night?"

"Yes, the neighbors, it's all they've been talking about."

"Well it seems the fire was started deliberately by someone, and inside we've discovered two bodies."

"Oh my God, do you think it might be my girls?" Sheila started to cry.

Steve stepped into the doorway, put his arm around her, and walked her to the sitting room. He made her sit down, and crouched on his heels in front of her and tactfully explained.

"Listen, the bodies were badly burned, beyond recognition, we don't really know who it is yet. It's just that when you called me earlier, and said they didn't come back; I just wanted to prepare you, in case it is the twins. We have to run some tests on the bodies first, and we will know more in a couple of days, if in the meantime they do come back then call me, I am sorry to come here and upset you with this, but I thought you should know first."

"I will call Jim and tell him, he's away right now, but he will contact the station to get the details, if we don't hear from you before."

Steve left Sheila in the flat and went back down to his car; he decided to take the stairs down saving him from that god-awful smell. He didn't feel very good about the news he'd just given. Deep down he knew that it might be the Jones girls; he was determined to catch the killer, he walked slowly down the stairwell contemplating his next task.

At the lab, Shabby was studiously scouring the dental records, on the x-ray box there were two sets of teeth; they were both identical, even down to the curl on the left front incisor. He squinted through his glasses, and he knew that they belonged to the twins; his assistant had appeared behind him.

"The Coroner has phoned through his report, the cause of death was smoke inhalation and eighty to a hundred percent burns, and as you already knew, they were burnt alive."

Shabby peered at her, he made a motion, rolling his arm over and pointed to a chair, and she sat next to him at his desk.

"I have no doubt that the bodies are of the Jones twins, the teeth are identical. There are clear signs that they were tied up when the fire started, they suffered badly before they finally died, there isn't a trace of evidence left on them, this killer was very careful not to leave any fibres behind, if he did leave any then the fire took care of that, but we have this card with writing on and we've deciphered 'OUR CLOTHES ON', we should get more from the specialist lab in the City. I also believe this person knew the girls, but who the hell it was I don't know yet, and I reckon they were probably targeted on purpose."

His assistant plucked the x-rays off the light box and placed them back in the file. Shabby and Sara went to study the bodies for themselves, and left the labs for the mortuary. When they entered the mortuary, the smell that greeted them was abundant with smoke. They put on robes and masks, which would allow them to get close to the bodies, without feeling nauseous. The bodies of the twins were lying side by side, toe tags weren't put on yet, and that job fell to Shabby. He was certain that it was Betty and Caitlin, and wrote their names out, then Sara began to tie the tags to the twins' toes, she paused to say.

"Which is which? I'm not sure."

Shabby shrugged and replied, with logic.

"Usually identical twins would stand in an order of their birth, enabling people to know which twin they were talking to, so let's put Betty's name on the toe to the left and Caitlin on the right, then hope we've got it correct."

Shabby left Sara to work for a few moments, and he went to phone Steve, and give him the bad news. Steve was at the station when the call came through; he picked up the phone, his gut turned over as he held the receiver to his ear.

"It's your worst fears Steve, it is the twins, you won't like this bit either. There is nothing off the bodies or the surrounding area at the scene. We can't find any evidence whatsoever; we might never find who killed them."

Steve stared blankly for a moment, before giving a reply.

"I will find something, that's a promise. Tell Mr Jones when he calls you? He will want to know it's his daughters, I'm going for a drive to clear my head." As he put down the phone Paul Collison came into the office, he was waving a piece of paper.

"I've been out to question some of the locals, apparently on Saturday night a few of them saw a person acting strangely near the scene before it burnt down, I have written down the description for you."

"Tell me, what is it?"

"A few of them saw a man or woman dressed in a long black coat, with the hood up. They never saw the face, it was covered up with something, the locals thought it looked out of place, but not suspicious."

"Good, we have something to look for, pin the notes up on the board, next to the photographs of the bodies; we'll get the crime artist to make an impression of what they've seen." Steve left the office to go for his drive.

Back at the mortuary, Shabby had returned to help Sara. They only had two hours to study the twins, before the undertakers came to lay them in the chapel of rest. Shabby worked on the body to his left first, using his instruments to carefully remove the rest of the clothing, the top she wore is part polyester and some pieces were lodged in the skin when they'd melted. There was a large section in the centre of the body, which Shabby peeled off carefully, underneath was untouched perfect skin, he looked at Sara and spoke.

"Make sure when the embalmers work on these two, that the skin looks as perfect as this."

Sara photographed the strip of skin, and continued with her work on the other body. There weren't any clothes on this one; all the skin was burnt off.

"These girls weren't given a chance, whoever killed them wanted them to suffer. Right we'll finish up here and then the embalmers can come in and get them ready."

When Jim Jones got home, Sheila went to him and held him for a long while, he'd been working away, so would not have known about his daughters. Jim was an ordinary hardworking man, and he's the same age as Sheila. Jim isn't much to look at but he is well off financially working in Corporate Real Estate. He kissed Sheila and noticed her looking upset.

"Oh Jim, I want you to sit down, there's been some bad news you see."

Jim took off his jacket and sat in his armchair, and she sat on an arm to continue divulging the bad news.

"There was a fire last night at The Barn, it was caught on fire deliberately, and the police think that Betty and Caitlin were in there."

"What are you trying to tell me Sheila?"

"They think they may be dead, our girls are gone Jim." Sheila became hysterical.

"Are they sure it's Bet and Cait, how do they know?" Jim started to weep.

Sheila tried to search for the right words to say, without making things worse.

"They never came back last night love, and they still haven't come home even now. They went to The Barn for a party, and now you know about the fire." Sheila cried again and left the sitting room, she returned with tissues and handed some so Jim.

"I can't believe we'll never see them again, who did this to us I don't understand?" Jim was becoming angrier by the second.

"The police don't know, you need to call the station and speak to them, maybe they've got leads by now."

Jim went to telephone the station, and he needed answers. Simon picked up the call, and was already armed with the information from Shabby.

"This is Jim Jones. I am calling you for information about my daughters, Betty and Caitlin, could you help me?"

Simon drew in some breath and began replying to Jim's request.

"The Pathologist has identified two bodies found at The Barn Nightclub, and they are of your daughters, I am afraid, they're being processed so that you can formally identify them yourselves, so if you can please call into the mortuary at your earliest convenience and do this for us?"

Jim paused so that he could compose himself, and then spoke again.

"Do you know who it was that attacked our girls, any reasons why they were targeted?"

Simon wanted to give Jim some good news, but knew there wasn't any.

"We don't have anything to tell you on that front, sorry Mr Jones, the officers are working tirelessly to find you some answers." Simon felt bad; well at least he tried.

"Thank you for letting us know, we will be along later to see the girls for ourselves," Jim hung up the phone.

Sheila and Jim held each other while they let out their grief, knowing the full extent of their daughters' ordeal. When their upset subsided; the thought of going to see their children no longer living, suddenly dawned on them. They got ready to go; Sheila changed her clothes and Jim waited for her to finish. The drive over meant that they passed the burnt building; their daughters had been trapped in. Jim stopped and looked at it for a few moments and then pulled away, to continue driving to the mortuary. Simon had called in advance, allowing Shabby a bit of time to organize their viewing. When Jim and Sheila arrived Shabby came to greet them personally.

"Mr and Mrs Jones, my condolences to you both at this tragic time, we need to explain a few things before we proceed, so with your permission can we go in here and speak?" Jim nodded and followed Shabby into the room with Sheila, and waited to hear what he was going to say.

"When we were called to the scene, your daughters were severely burnt, to such an extent that Caitlin had no skin left; it had all been burnt off. The embalmers have done their best with them, so you can at least see the twins as you remember them, and say your goodbyes."

Jim and Sheila were holding hands and gripped each other's tightly, after Shabby's speech.

"So, if you could follow me please and remember they lie in a delicate state so please, I know it will be hard, but try not to touch them?"

Jim and Sheila followed Shabby along the corridor to the double doors at the end, and he held one open to allow them in and closed it behind once they were through. Their daughters were laid out in front of them, sheets covered them from the neck down, and they looked pristine.

"They look like they're sleeping." Sheila began to cry again. Jim turned away and ran back out of the doors and away from the mortuary, leaving Sheila there, he couldn't take it all. Shabby had to bring her home later.

"You understand that they can't be released until this case is solved, Mrs Jones?"

He watched Sheila leave his car, and then disappear into the block of flats. Jim hadn't got home yet from the mortuary, he was sitting where his girls used to play in the park, when they were little. He was swinging on Caitlin's favourite swing, and the roundabout was turning. He was imagining his girls were playing here and he was watching. He couldn't control his tears, as the magnitude of the moment finally sunk in; earlier that day he had closed a massive deal, meaning a small windfall was coming, enough to feel comfortable for the rest of his life. How had it all gone wrong, from a day of absolute elation, to one of utter devastation, in just ten hours?

Chapter 3

The Ritual of Richard Joiner.

The next day Jim and Sheila were at the pub, telling all the punters news about Betty and Caitlin, everyone was stunned, they all knew how popular the twins were in the village; they had won beauty pageants year after year. The twins' murder could take a while to solve, and there wasn't a release date for the girls, so they couldn't even arrange their funerals. Nobody knew who had the women killed, and the whole inquiry could take such a long time. Just then a couple walked over to Jim and Sheila, it was Richard Joiner and Cathy French. Ricky and Cathy had been dating for nearly twenty-five years, but never married, because of his commitment to the Army, it was thought Cathy didn't want to pressure him into marriage, she was happy with their arrangement. Richard spent years pursuing his career and Cathy was proud of his dedication to his country. He had even received the Queen's Gallantry Medal, for valour in the field of combat. He was wearing his army uniform, and looked like a giant compared to his shorter girlfriend, who was dressed in a black trouser suit. Cathy put her arm through Sheila's and they stood together as Richard came over to them, and spoke in his usual deep voice.

"I'm sorry for your loss Jim; I have been granted leave from my unit, so if there is anything I can do for you, then just call."

Jim nodded in silence, too grief stricken to talk. He was completely devastated by this, almost suicidal.

"Any idea who it was that killed them?" Richard asked.

"No, the cops have nothing to go on so far," said Sheila.

"They were in The Barn right, that rings a bell but I can't pin point it right this moment."

"Come on Ricky, let's leave it hey? We can question this later." Cathy tried soothing the tension.

Richard had a bit of an idea about who it might be, but kept that inside, he didn't want to reveal what the girls did to Outlaw; that night of the firework incident, the timing would be too insensitive; so he did what Cathy asked.

As Richard's mother and father ran the pub, it was decided that they would host a memorial wake there the following Wednesday in honour of the twins.

Wednesday came by and before the party everyone placed flowers at the scene of their death, there were hundreds of bouquets, the whole pub was packed out with support for Jim and Sheila. Steve was at the pub trying to see if anybody there was acting smug or unemotional, perhaps he could get some clues. The task was difficult, as people were either crying into handkerchiefs or embracing each other, and he couldn't really see their faces. He decided to leave, made his excuses to Jim and Sheila. The villagers enjoyed a dignified service at the pub, giving the twins a loving send-off playing a batch of their favourite songs and family members were giving emotional speeches. People were asking why were the twins killed like this, but nobody had answers. Some were getting too drunk to rationally think straight, and a few fights broke out, blaming small incidences that the twins had with certain families. Raymond Joiner, the Landlord, broke up the fighting, rang the bell for last orders, and then shut for the afternoon.

Later that night Richard was in the kitchen of his house, he was pouring his coffee. Cathy had taken off her jacket, and then joined Richard in the kitchen. The photo album that she was carrying, was put on the dining table, she went to the kitchen sink and stood there quietly. She was staring out of the window into the back garden, she could see Betty and Caitlin's place, and she was remembering all the things they did as kids, the first time they all met, back at High School, how she wanted to be their friends, because of their popularity. That is how she met Richard; everything else flowed from then on. The foursome became such strong friends, that they even went skinny dipping together, as if it were the most natural thing to do. Cathy felt sorry that they didn't catch up one last time. Richard approached her and wrapped his strong arms around her, he began stroking her shoulders, which she found comforting, he kissed the back of her neck and she pushed backwards allowing his kissing to continue. Having Richard at home made Cathy feel safer about things; if somebody killed her friends, would they try and come for us? At least with him here, whoever it was would have to think twice, she thought. Richard moved her from the sink and sat her down at the table and she began to leaf through the photo album. He then went to change into more casual clothes. When Richard returned, Cathy laid her head in her hands and began to cry.

"I can't believe they're gone. Who do you think it was, then Ricky?" She asked him in mid cry; he walked over to Cathy when he noticed she was upset.

"There was this time when Betty and Caitlin had asked me to go with them; because they wanted to play a trick on that kid, Outlaw. This was over twenty years ago though. I got him into a choke-hold for them, while they tied him up with a rope. Then I lifted him up and left him hanging there, the girls then asked me to leave after that. Later when I saw them, they told me that they had tied a firework to his cock and lit it, and they kind of found it funny. When I found out; went back there to the barn and cut the poor beggar down again. I've done my own share of picking on him in the past."

"Outlaw died, didn't he? The family have told everyone the day he disappeared," Cathy refused to believe what Richard was telling her.

"Yeah, but the twins' bodies were found at The Barn right? And these events are kind of similar to that time; you know fireworks and hay bales?"...

(flashback)

Richard and Gerard had a lot of history in the past before he disappeared. Richard had always been obsessed with guns and the army, he would torment Gerard at every opportunity he could. Richard had a group of mates he would go around with at school, wherever he went, they would follow, like Luke Jarvis, he was a stocky and well-dressed boy. There was also Jeremy Stanley or Jez, as he liked to be called. He's a Cousin of Richard, he is tall, strong and athletic. Jez spent most of his time, fueling Richard's obsession with guns by taking him to the local Paintball Centre. Jez was one of the marshals, and worked there on weekends. Lastly there was Colin Rusdale; he was Richard's best friend at school. Colin was the bad influence on them all. It was Richard who was the most popular out of them though. There was a time at school, where after physical education; they would whip Gerard's naked body with wet towels, in the boys changing rooms. Most boys in their time at school, have experienced wet towel fights, but not to this extent. They would all whip at him, until Gerard was red and stinging with pain. This would be done every time they took P.E together. They would stop when Coach came to the rescue and saved him, all he would say was:

"You've got to stick up for yourself Swales, or they will do this all the time."

That was easier said than done, when you've got four strong boys after you, he thought. Another time; when Richard and Jez were on the way to their usual weekend session of skirmish, they spied Gerard walking through the woods; and lay in ambush ready to grab him. They threw a wool bag over his head and frogmarched him to the paintball centre. Richard lifted him across the fence in a fireman's carry. They took the bag off and Gerard stood squinting for a moment. He realized there were eight people all pointing their paintball guns at him. Always the ringleader; Colin Rusdale started the teasing.

"Hey Outlaw! We need some target practise, being that this is the first game of the season."

Gerard wanted to run but when he tried to, he fell to the ground because Jez had tied his bootlaces together. Then Luke Jarvis joined in.

"What do you reckon Ricky, points for the body and extra balls if you are consistent?"

"Yep, sounds good to me."

They all just started to shoot their guns at Gerard; every single shot hit him on the body and legs, stinging him intensely like a swarm of bees.

"Shit! I'm empty." Luke was frustrated, and threw his gun to the ground in disgust. The other boys carried on shooting at Gerard; Colin was the next to be empty followed by two other people in the group, Stu and Zach. They were both of black African origin, and were sporty, competitive young men.

"Not consistent enough to refill," ruled Jez.

He sat down holding his gun; he looked on with enthusiasm as Richard emptied all his paint-balls, on target into Gerard's chest.

"I won't refill, I've done enough - come on let's go then?" Richard gave the order and they all walked casually away, leaving Gerard covered in paint, sobbing on the ground alone.

The final time Richard had a run-in with Gerard, was at a party, Richard caught him looking at Cathy, while she was dancing to music. He gathered his buddies up, so that he could exact his punishment on Gerard. They had all been drinking heavily that night. The boys dragged him from where he was sitting, to the shed at the end of the garden. Richard was sat at a table; the others pushed Gerard in and forced him to sit down. Luke and Colin held him in a sitting position. Jez came from behind Richard; he was holding a pistol, and it was a Colt 45. He spun the barrel, clicked it open, and then handed the gun to Richard. Richard roared at Gerard in his deepest voice.

"You want a piece of my girlfriend, there's one way that you can earn your right to try." Richard was inspecting the bullet chamber of the pistol. He placed an empty casing in the gun, faking putting a bullet in the barrel and snapped it shut; spun the barrel, and he cocked the hammer back.

"There are five of us here right, so we take it in turns, point the gun to our heads and pull the trigger. If the chamber is empty and you live, you may leave this shed and have a go at Cathy." Gerard shook his head in disagreement; Colin and Luke increased their hold on him.

"There's no choice Outlaw, we're all going to do this, whether you like it or not."

Richard put the gun to his temple and looked straight at Gerard and smiled, he pulled the trigger and he blinked briefly as the hammer clicked, but no bullet came out. Gerard trembled with fear. Richard handed the gun to Jez, who cocked it again, put the gun to his head and pulled the trigger. Nothing again, he laughed crazily as the gun was handed to Luke, who had swapped places with Jez, holding Gerard down. Luke quickly took his turn, with the same outcome; he swapped back with Jez, who handed the gun to Colin. Colin squeezed the trigger, again no shot. The gun was passed back to Richard; he had a second go.

"Last one is yours Outlaw, you must fire the gun or my mates will do it for you, as this is a six-shooter; and five shots have been fired, this means the bullet is still in here. Take the shot, and if you survive then Cathy is all yours." Gerard was shaking; he knew the gun would kill him.

"Do it!" Richard bellowed.

Gerard slowly lifted the gun to his head and waited a moment; tears were streaming down his face, he squeezed the trigger, the gun clicked, but no bullet came out, the two men holding him, pulled him down, the back of the chair slammed to the floor, Gerard banged his head as the floor of the shed was hard. Richard came around to Gerard and leaned over him.

"As if I would let a worm like you; get anywhere near Cathy, you're such an arsehole! If you ever look at her again that way, there will be bullets in this gun, got it!"

Gerard stayed lying on the shed floor a good ten minutes, shaking with fright after the boys had left.

When Richard first joined the army, he realized very quickly that he was the pipsqueak, the new boy that all his comrades would have a go at. After a while the initiations made a man of him, he also realized that what he had done to Gerard in the past was appalling, but regretted the chance to apologize for what he'd put him through. That last incident with Gerard was twenty-two years ago to this day...

(present)

It is Thursday morning and Richard got up early to go for his daily run; Cathy rolled over in the bed; it felt snug and warm, but as she awoke noticed the big space Richard had left behind, she reached around to feel him, but he wasn't there. Richard had disappeared out of the house for his jog. She rose and got dressed slowly, looking in the mirror at herself as she did so, Cathy was proud of her figure and loved to see herself cover it up, she took a purple t-shirt out of a chest of drawers, she returned to the mirror to put it on, she pulled it down over her slowly and sensually, with no bra on under it, she could see her nipples poking through. The bottom half of her was still naked, Cathy moved closer to the mirror as she studied her legs and thighs, Cathy went back to the drawers and took some white shorts out, she came back to the mirror carrying them, and watched herself as she just slid the shorts up slowly. Richard was Cathy's one and only love, so this would be nice for Richard, when he returned from his run. Cathy would spend, as much time as she could with him, while he was home, their sexual appetite never waned. He would need a shower and Cathy would join him, when he got back. The less she had to take off, the better for them both. Cathy finished dressing and she walked downstairs to prepare some breakfast. While Richard was out jogging, he decided to take a short cut through the Carmellen Park; he was playing music through his portable player and his running pace matched the rhythm, he continued his run along the main road; and down the farm lane to the large woods at the bottom, he turned into the woods and ran along a footpath. He took the left fork in the path and his pace was starting to slow, he ran down the steep path towards the stream. To his left a figure dressed in a black shiny coat flashed through the trees, sprinting very rapidly, then disappeared again. Richard felt unnerved for a second, but brushed it off after a couple of paces. His run took him parallel to the paintball centre and again, this time to his right; a black-coated figure flashed through the fir trees. This time he did stop running and started walking over to what he had seen. He was breathing heavily and because of this, he didn't hear somebody coming up behind him. He felt a very heavy blow to the back of his head and he blacked out completely. Richard came to, and noticed he was inside the paintball zone, in one of the huts. His head was pounding from the blow he'd received. Straight away he knew that he was tied to something. Just as he was getting his bearings, a voice came from a tape recording, a voice he'd never heard before.

"Good morning Ricky," it began. "As you now know, you are tied to a chair, as a kid this was your favourite place to go. Your legs and ankles are lashed together; and your body is bound tightly."

The figure that he had seen in the woods stood with its arms folded, leaning against the bolted door.

"Tied between your legs and feet is a double-barrelled shotgun. This is pointing at your face. The gun is primed and ready to fire, should you move your legs suddenly, the string will pull the trigger and the gun will fire, it will shoot you straight in the face." The voice paused for a second. Richard kept his legs still as he could. The figure moved from the door and sat on a barrel opposite Richard.

"Just for good measure, your arms are tied behind you, and there is a cross bow secured to the floor. This is pointing up to the back of your head; the bolt is set ready to fire too. If you are tempted to move your arms, the cross bow will fire, the bolt will go into your head and once again you will die."

The tightness of the binds on Richard's arms made him realize how serious his aggressor was.

"This is how it is Ricky, whether you are awake, and you make sudden movements, either weapon will kill you. Should you fall asleep and perhaps relax, the weapons will fire, and of course the same outcome. Such dilemmas to be in hey Ricky? But if you feel like staying still, then you will just starve to death, see how long it will be before someone notices you're missing, how's your luck?"

The voice had ended and the figure got up from the barrel, unbolted the door, and as it left, wedged something against the outside of the door. Richard could hear the figure walking away; he sat still for a moment, and he thought of Cathy briefly, the day they met way back in the first year at school. This made him feel better about things for a brief while. He was the first person she ever kissed, and the only person she ever had sex with, he was remembering their first time together, she was so loving and knew exactly what he liked, they had spent so many years together and hardly ever rowed, they had mild disagreements, but nothing ever made them split up.

Richard's life was never complicated; he always had a carefree attitude. This situation he was in was nothing compared to what he had been involved in previously. He contemplated his life so far, and came to a conclusion; he had been enriched by his love for Cathy, and her love for him, he thought of her left behind after he was gone. He thought of the career path he had chosen, in the army he had fought for his country, places like, Kosovo, Iraq and Afghanistan, he never got caught out, wounded or became a prisoner, for his heroics rose to the rank of Major. He always knew he would die before he was fifty, a psychic medium told him that once.

Richard came to a conclusion, that he was going to die right here and now, he wanted the quickest exit he could get. He made up his mind and with one swift movement, pulled his arms and legs together, as this happened the shotgun and cross bow both fired, Richard's face was ripped apart by the blast from the shot gun, the force of the kick back had dislocated his knees, and shattered both ankles. The crossbow bolt fired upwards and pierced the back of Richard's head, going straight through his brain. This made Richard grunt as it entered, and he felt no pain. The shotgun had thrown Richard backwards onto the floor; and the chair he was sitting on was smashed to pieces, and he just lay still. Richard Joiner died instantly.

Chapter 4

Never a Dull Moment.

It was ten o'clock by now, Cathy was starting to get concerned, the fried breakfast she had cooked turned cold. Richard usually ran for no more than two hours, by this time it was nearly four. She picked up her mobile and phoned his number, sometimes he dropped in on Jez on the way back and sometimes he brought Jez back with him, she hoped that today he'd be alone; it was his hard, fit body that she wanted so badly. The phone connected straight to his voicemail, she threw the mobile onto the settee, suddenly her mobile rang, the number withheld. She picked it up and listened.

"Hi! Cathy, its Jez, is the old boy up yet?"

"Oh, Jez help me, I think something bad may have happened to him."

"Why do you think that, is he there or not?"

"He got up at six this morning as normal to go for his jog, you know he runs, right? Well it's ten now and he only normally takes two hours. He hasn't come back yet." Cathy started to cry.

"Look, I'll come over with my car, okay and we'll go look for him." The phone cut off, Cathy went and got ready to go out. Fifteen minutes later, Jez's car pulled up outside the house. Cathy put her coat on and walked out of the door.

"This doesn't feel right Jez; he's never late for anything," said Cathy as she got in.

"Yeah, I know what you mean, babes. Where shall we look first?"

"He usually runs along the main road and then a long circuit back through the woods, and back past your place." Cathy revealed.

"Okay then, we'll drive there and start looking."

He started his car, began to drive through the estate and down to the main road. After a few minutes, he pulled the car up on the verge, so that he was off the road. They stepped out of the car and began their walk down the farm lane, leading to the woods. Jez squatted for a moment, and peered at the muddy ground in front of him.

"Yep, he definitely went this way look, he's wearing his bloody great army boots, and only a yeti has feet that size." Jez said, pointing at the size twelve footprints on the ground.

"Let's follow them then?"

They began following the huge stride of footprints down the lane; they reached the entrance to the woods and stopped for a few minutes.

"Which way do you think he ran?" The footprints had disappeared off the path, leaving them confused. Jez tried to reassure Cathy.

"Look, I know these woods as well as Ricky right; I bet he ran down to the stream and along the path beside the paintball centre."

"Right, you're the leader?"

They both went into the woods and walked the way they thought he might have run. They had reached the stream, and stopped for a moment; Jez crossed over the bridge and looked at the footpath on the other side.

"No footprints here; he didn't go this way, I bet I was right first time and he cut up by the west fence, come on?"

They walked away from the stream and up to the other path, leading to the paintball centre. Ten minutes later they reached a fence; pieces of it were lying on the ground.

"Hey, this fence is broken, look."

As a full-time marshal at the paintball centre, Jez knew it had to have been damaged this morning. He'd made his fence checks last thing yesterday, and they were all fine then.

"Right, let's go in here?"

Cathy and Jez crossed the fence and walked through the fir trees and out the other side, they reached the pontoon, part of the water section at the paintball centre. The paintball centre has five sections, tall grassland, and open terrain, fox holes, water and desert zones. Jez pointed to the hut, fifty yards over on the right-hand side; it had a plank wedged against the door.

"Over there!" Jez had a sudden urge to whisper.

They walked up to the hut with an impending sense of doom. Jez moved the plank away and opened the door. He looked in and immediately vomited. Richard was lying on the floor, blood all over the place, his face torn apart.

"Cathy, don't look."

She swept by him and looked in screaming.

"Don't go in! The scene needs to be left as it is for the police." Jez shouted, but he was still being sick.

Cathy started to cry hysterically, and Jez held her away from the hut.

"I want to hold him." She could see it was her Ricky even though his face was shredded from the shot.

"You can't touch him, you will contaminate the place; look I'll call the police on my mobile."

He was trying to be strong for Cathy's sake, but inside he was just as distraught as her. Jez called the police and Paul Collison answered.

"Mortal Dean Police. Sergeant Collison speaking."

"This is Jeremy Stanley; I am at the paintball centre. I have found my cousin, Richard Joiner. He's dead, his face is blown apart, and there's blood everywhere." Jez sounded like he was panicking, and Paul tried to calm him.

"Right okay, stay there please and I will call my colleagues and join you just, soon as we can."

"Bring a female officer, will you? His girlfriend is with me, and she's in a bad way."

"No problem Mr Stanley hang tight, we'll sort it all out for you." The conversation ended and Collison called Steve's office.

"Steve; another killing this time it's Richard Joiner, he's been shot, up at the paintball centre, it sounds like a game gone wrong or something."

"Right I'll call Shabby at home, get him in, where is this scene?"

"The fellow on the phone said in the storage hut on the left of the entrance to the paintball centre."

Steve dialed his phone and called Shabby.

"Shabs; we might have another bloody murder." Steve said this with an air of frustration.

"Oh, no not more, we haven't finished with the last lot! Right, where, who, when?"

"Paintball centre, a male named Richard Joiner, in the hut by the entrance," Steve replied.

"Three in a week, feels like we are going to have our hands full here," said Shabby.

"I'll meet you there, okay," said Steve, and hung up the phone, glared over at his incident board and walked out of the office to his car.

Twenty minutes later he arrived at the car park of the paintball centre, he was met by Shabby as he got out. Jez was waiting at the walk-through to the hut; Cathy was sitting on a log, her face hidden in her coats high collar trying to conceal her crying. The police wagon, Paul Collison at the wheel with PC Cheryl Cleats followed him into the car park; Collison pulled the wagon alongside Steve's Mercedes.

"Right Steve, we will have a look at the scene together," Shabby took command.

The two men walked down to the where Jez was waiting, Collison ran to catch up and Cheryl walked over to Cathy. She was carrying a blanket and a flask of hot tea. The blanket she placed over Cathy's shoulders and drew her arm around her and she held her tightly. Cathy started to cry again, this time uncontrollably. Jez led Steve, Shabby and Paul down to the hut, where Richard's body lay. Shabby went inside first; he put on some purple latex gloves, and handed a pair to Steve.

"Right Paul, stay outside please? Don't let anyone past the door until Steve and I are finished, okay?"

"No problem, Shabs."

Paul stepped back to allow Steve entry, and he stood with his back to the door.

"This is overkill, very efficient; the killer definitely wanted him dead..." Was Shabby's opening observation.

He took out a white lollipop stick looking device; on one side were millimetre measurements. He lined up the stick beside the remains of Richard's face. He took out his notebook and wrote down what he had measured. Steve knelt next to Shabby and examined the shotgun between Richard's legs.

"There's still one shot left in here."

"Good, we may get some prints off the cartridge; we'll take both weapons back with us and run a full ballistics report."

Steve looked up for a moment and noticed a small cassette recorder in the corner of the hut. He stood up and walked over to it; he pulled out a clear evidence bag, and placed it inside. He went over to Paul, still waiting by the door.

"Here, take this to the van, will you?"

Paul took the bag from Steve and walked to the van. Steve went back into the hut; Shabby was making audio notes of Richard's injuries.

"His legs are shattered and displaced by the shotgun recoil; he has presumably been knocked backwards by the blast. The crossbow bolt in the back of his head, is actually keeping his skull together. No doubt he died instantaneously. Time of death, between seven and eight this morning, the extent of stiffness in the corpse suggests he's been lying here for approximately four to five hours." He clicked off his Dictaphone and put it back in his pocket.

"Right Shabs, time to get the body back to the lab and inform the Coroner."

While they waited for that to happen, they continued their investigation. Steve left the hut for a minute and went over to Jez and sat him down for a talk.

"You found him here? You're his cousin right; do you know who might have done this to him?"

"Can't think of anything right now Detective; I'm too numb to give you any names."

"Okay, we'll need a formal full statement from you later."

Jez was sick again, as Steve turned away. Shabby came out of the hut and lit a cigarette.

"If this is linked to the first case; we may have a serial killer here in Mortal Dean." Shabby puffed out the smoke.

"Then we must find that link, Shabs."

The Coroner's van came into the car park and stopped alongside the walk-through; he got out and opened the back of his wagon. His co-driver came with him pushing the stretcher in front of him. Moments later they appeared with Richard's body, a black plastic zip up bag covered it; they slowly wheeled it up the slope and carried him into the back of the wagon. Cathy was watching this and went over to Jez; he held her close as the wagon pulled away from the scene. She buried her face into his chest and cried again. Cheryl went over again to give her comfort. Shabby waved Steve and Paul over to where he was standing. They went to him without hesitation.

"This hut is transportable, we can lift the whole thing up and take it to the labs, and we can work with it there, instead of trudging down here all the time."

"Right, I'll arrange for it to be lifted," Paul offered.

They all walked to their vehicles, except Steve who turned to face Cathy.

"We are going to find his killer, Miss French, I promise you."

Cathy nodded in acceptance and she left with Jez, who took her home. Steve and Shabby milled around for a while, waiting for the crane and low-loader for the hut to arrive. Paul and Cheryl headed back to the station.

It is Friday and Cathy is at the house; starting to sort out Richard's belongings, going through her mind were the thoughts about her friends, Betty and Caitlin, killed only a week ago, all their prettiness gone, burnt off. She hadn't seen her friends for four years; she couldn't believe they were dead. And now Ricky, slaughtered without any consideration for her. She didn't want to think about who it was, but she would like to get her hands on the killer, for ruining her life like this. Cathy screwed up the jumper she was holding, as she dwelt on that thought for a moment. With Richard's body at the mortuary, she knew it would be a while before the police would release him, so that she could arrange his funeral. Keeping busy like this, it would take her mind off it all. She stopped to pour a gin from the drinks bureau; she didn't normally drink this early but nobody would blame her, for taking the edge off things for a while. Cathy finished her drink and wiped the dribbles off her chin. Tears came to her eyes again, and she cleared them off with her hand and put the glass down; then she continued packing up Richard's clothes. There was a ring on her doorbell; it was Jez, and he'd changed his clothes, had a wash and didn't smell of sick any more, much to Cathy's relief.

"Jez, why is this happening to us?" She held tightly onto Jez, and he walked her into the kitchen.

"You feel like the whole world is against you, don't you?" He sat Cathy down at the dining table and went to make coffee, and he stated the obvious.

"We must call his Unit; tell them that he won't be coming back after leave."

"Yes, could you do that? I don't think I am strong enough to tell anyone that he's gone, just yet."

"No problem," Jez put down the coffees, and set about doing that.

He went to the phone; sifted through Richard's address book, and he found the number of Richard's Commanding Officer. He dialed the number and began delivering his bad news. Cathy gulped down the coffee so quickly, she was too numb to realize how hot it was. She carried on sorting out Richard's personal effects. Jez came into the lounge and started helping Cathy fold his clothes into a large suitcase.

"The cops phoned me this morning, they want us to go to the station, they want to question us, and asked if you feel up to answering any?"

"All I know is that Richard is dead and some bastard out there killed him, what a fucking coward!"

Jez looked down for a moment; he was shocked to hear Cathy swear that way, when she never normally would. He knew that he wouldn't get much more sense out of her.

"Right, I'll go, I've got to be there for two o'clock, will you be okay?"

Cathy nodded but didn't say anything; she was shocked that she had sworn too. Jez left her at the house to give his statement.

Back at the mortuary lab; Shabby was studying Richard's body more closely; he was wearing a mask and leaning across to look at his injuries. Steve was at the lab also; he was looking at the tape recorder in the evidence bag. He took it out for a listen; Steve leaned forward as the tape crackled into sound. As it played his face formed many expressions, the recording finished and he clicked off the play button, still wearing his gloves he placed the recorder back into the bag. Steve walked over to Shabby.

"Well the killer definitely knew him, he called him Ricky; he also knew him as a kid, because he referred to the place he was found at as his favourite. The voice was distorted though; it wasn't a naturally spoken tone, like it was disguised by some kind of voice changing device."

"The perpetrator doesn't want to be recognized; it also sounds like he was enjoying the crime. This makes me think that the killer was involved with the Jones' deaths too." Said Shabby.

"Right, so you are more certain than ever that we may have a serial killer here?" Steve asked.

"Not one killer, maybe somebody is helping him. Have you seen how big this guy is? He's nearly six foot five. He was probably unconscious when he was tied up; I've found evidence of a contusion on the back of his head and there isn't signs of any struggling. Maybe somebody else was with him to help 'cos the equipment would have taken a while to set up. Has anybody seen any suspicious people hanging around the area?"

Steve made notes of Shabby's findings and continued with his study of the weapons. The phone rang and Shabby's assistant answered it, she nodded a few times, and then replaced the receiver. She came over to Shabby and took off her glasses.

"There are no fingerprints on the cartridge of the shotgun, and none on the cross bow or bolt. There aren't any fibres on the ropes that he was tied with and there is nothing from the killer, just like the first murder."

"Damn it!" Steve vented his disgust, as he joined them.

"He must be wearing something that doesn't leave fibres behind, obviously wearing gloves, and there aren't any skin or hair particles on the body." Shabby was mapping out in his mind what could happen, and he pieced it all together.

"Three bodies so far, no evidence left behind, this person doesn't want to be caught at all"

"Well they're going to slip up soon, and when they do, we'll nail them." Steve was fidgeting angrily. "I've got to go back to the station; his cousin who discovered the body is coming in for his statement at two, call me if you find anything?"

Shabby nodded as Steve left the lab; then turned to continue his deliberations.

Steve came to the driveway of the police station; he parked in his space and sat for a moment. He banged the steering wheel with his fists in frustration and then got out of the car. As he entered the police station, he looked at Jez who was sat waiting for him.

"Thanks for coming to see us Jeremy, I know it must be hard for you, I am sorry for your loss." Jez stood up and followed Steve into his office. Simon was waiting for them there.

"Anything I can get you both?" He asked.

"Just two coffees and some cigarettes please Simon?"

Steve turned to his left and into the interview room; Paul Collison was already in the room, Steve started the introductions.

"This is Sgt. Collison, he'll be with us while we conduct your statement, and I'm Detective Steve Speed."

"Right, take a seat Jeremy." Collison pointed to the chair opposite him.

"Thanks, is this right being in here? It feels like I'm under arrest or something."

"Nonsense lad; just sit down, it's easier to come in here to talk, and we don't want people coming in and disturbing us, do we hey?"

With Jez at ease they both took their seats, to begin the session. Steve closed the door and joined them at the table.

"Tell us what you know about earlier today, please Mr Stanley?"

"Well this morning I called Ricky's house to see if he was there; he's home on leave from the army. He normally runs for two hours, sometimes ending up at my place, or sometimes he calls me up and takes me to his house. Well I rang Cathy; as he hadn't called in, and when she told me he wasn't there either, we became worried. I went over, picked her up and we started looking for him. She was panicking that something bad might have happened to him. After all, we were all upset about Betty and Caitlin being killed, Ricky and Cathy were best friends of theirs, inseparable as kids. I think it had hit him really hard, we thought maybe he needed time to clear his head; after that we went to the woods, because that is where he usually runs. We followed his footprints and found him at the paintball centre, which was about an hour later, and then we phoned you guys," explained Jez. Steve asked another question.

"Where were you between six and ten then Mr Stanley? All you're doing is explaining what happened after."

Jez looked at Steve; he was confused by his angle of questioning.

"I don't understand why do you want to know that?"

"Look, your cousin is dead, and your demeanour is kind of cool about that, so again I ask you, where did you go between six and ten this morning?"

"I was at my mates place, his name is Luke Jarvis okay; you can ask him if you don't believe me."

"We will Mr Stanley; thank you for your time, you can go now." Steve stood up and Collison scribbled down some information on the statement and pushed it towards Jez to sign, Jez signed it and left the room. Steve walked Jez out of the station, and came back into the incident room. He put the photograph taken of Richard; up alongside the one of the Jones'. He pointed at them and turned to Sgt. Collison, they walked out of the station and over to Steve's car, ready for their visit to the Carmellen estate.

"Right, let's see what this Luke Jarvis has to say, and see if he can back up this statement?" Collison commanded.

❈

Chapter 5

Concrete Alibi

Luke Jarvis has made a real name for himself, since leaving school. He went to a technical college to study building & construction. He completed his three-year apprenticeship, and then worked with local builders to start with; then he quickly grew into a skilled craftsman, and branched out on his own. The Mortal Dean residents would recommend him for any type of building contract. On this particular afternoon, he was working on his house. He'd spent the last ten years helping other people with their properties and his own home had always come second…

Before he left school though, he was just one of the lads, a bit of a layabout, albeit a smartly dressed one. Luke and Gerard never liked each other very much; right back to the day they started school together. That day, in his hurry to get to registration, Gerard accidentally tripped Luke over, as they rushed down the art block corridor. Luke went flying forward and slammed into Jez. Jez dropped his bag and began a scuffle with Luke. They fought for a while, whilst Gerard innocently hurried away. Sometime later Luke came into the classroom, he went over to Gerard's desk, he was red faced and panting, Jez had given him a real hiding. Gerard looked up at Luke, his left eye was starting to blacken, and his nose had a red mark on the bridge and his left nostril was bleeding a bit.

"See these bruises, they're your entire fault," Luke seethed. "I am going to make your life here as unbearable as I can," he vowed.

Gerard shrank back into his seat as Luke leaned over him before moving to his desk, further forward in the class, all the while staring back at Gerard, making his threat even more menacing. Later that day Luke visited Jez's class, to apologize and explain that it was Gerard who'd tripped him and that is why he fell on him. From that moment Jez and Luke became good friends. At the end of that first school day, the pair of them waited for

Gerard to come out of the school gates. As Gerard appeared, Luke rushed up to him, he got him into a headlock, with his left fist; punched Gerard in the sweet spot, right in the kidney, and Jez stood by, egging Luke on. Gerard staggered away holding his side; he was writhing with pain.

"That's just for starters Swales, you caused me trouble this morning, and I'm going to make you pay," promised Luke.

"Is that his name, Swales? We should call him Outlaw then, what do you reckon?" Jez asked.

"Good nickname Jez, from now on we will call you Outlaw Gerard Swales, or Outlaw for short," teased Luke.

They walked away from Gerard laughing; he was leaning on the fence trying to gather his breath, after the kidney punch he'd received.

From that moment on Gerard's life at school became a nightmare. He would wait, at the end of the day, for all the pupils to go home first, before making his way home by circuitous routes avoiding everybody. He would get home safely every school evening, but while he was in school, Luke, Jez, Richard and Colin would make his time there a complete hell. The week before they were due to leave school, Luke and Jez had planned a leaving present for Gerard. This called upon Richard and Colin for help; it involved staking out Gerard on the ground and pouring warm tar over him and then dropping feathers on top of the tar. They all waited eagerly for the final school bell. As it rang, all four boys raced to meet in the bus park; they could see all the school pupils leaving from there. They spotted Gerard coming out through the main hall and pass the buses. They followed behind him, making sure they weren't seen. They saw him turn down the lane towards his Dad's farm. They continued to follow him until he was half way down the lane; they all cheered and charged at him, the four boys running at Gerard, made him freeze to the spot, they managed to grab him, an arm and a leg each, his school bag went flying into the hedge. They carried him through the narrow pathway that led to a few barns at the back of the farm. Once inside one of the larger barns they found the machine that heats tar, further along the barn is a workshop, which Gerard's mother uses to make her bedding business, stuffing pillows and quilts with poultry feathers was a useful income. While Jez and Luke pegged out Gerard's arms and legs to the floor, Richard and Colin started heating the tar and then they gathered up the feathers, from the huge vat they were being stored in. They filled a bag, and moved the tar machine into place; the tar was warm enough to pour, so slowly they began to tip the chute down, some tar ran out and onto Gerard's feet, Colin and Richard moved away to allow Luke and Jez a turn to operate the machine. Luke pushed the machine along, so that the tar poured over Gerard's legs, he swapped with Jez who poured the tar over the waist and chest. Gerard lay wriggling on the ground as the warm tar started to cool and stiffen. Richard opened the bag of feathers and shook the whole lot into the air. The feathers began to fall and settle over Gerard's body, they stuck to the tar; they had fallen and landed all over Gerard, totally coating him from head to foot. The four boys left him lying there and ran off laughing, making clucking noises as they left. A few minutes later to Gerard's relief, he could hear his mother outside; she was calling some of the ducks for a feed.

"Mum, help!" He shouted.

Geraldine walked over to the barn, then went inside, and to her shock saw her son lying there, he was crying and looking at her with such a sad face. She cleaned him up and promised him that his father wouldn't hear about this incident. That was the final time Gerard 'Outlaw' Swales suffered any kind of torture, or humiliation, for at the end of that week he'd vanished, both his family, and the police, or anyone else for that matter, heard from him again...

This past month Luke had planned to build an extension on the back of his house, landscape his garden and re-lay the front driveway. The driveway was complete; the fences in the garden were taken away, the large hole made for the foundation to his extension, was ready to receive the concrete, around the inside of the hole he had laid bricks, to mark where the inner walls would be built, around the side path and slightly to the rear, a scaffolding platform had been erected, so that Luke could work on the roof. It was Friday afternoon, and Luke was sitting on a pile of tiles on his roof, he was taking a well-earned tea break. He was concerned that his cement was taking a while getting to him, so he used his mobile phone to quicken up the delivery.

"I don't know what you are doing, but I ordered concrete two hours ago, if it isn't delivered in the next ten minutes, then the whole lot will go off, and I'd have wasted my money," he bellowed down the receiver.

The girl on the other end remained as professional as she could, following Luke's barrage.

"We sent out the load at twelve o'clock this afternoon Sir, straight after your order," she replied.

"Oh right, I'm sorry then, there must be a problem with the lorry driver then," said Luke, feeling a little embarrassed about shouting at the girl.

"I will try and contact the driver from this end, to speed up your concrete Sir," she said.

He clicked off his phone, and as he looked over the apex of his roof, he could see the cement lorry coming through the estate at the top end. It was a while away yet, so he continued with the roof repairs.

The cement lorry had finally arrived at Luke's house, and the driver reversed it round, so that the back end was pointing over the foundation hole. Luke couldn't see the driver from his position on the roof, he had faith enough in him, not to interfere with his concrete pouring, and he continued with his work on the roof. The giant bowl on the back of the lorry, began to churn the cement inside, the driver let it turn for a few minutes, then pushed the chute over the hole and pulled the lever back, this allowed the concrete to slurp out and begin filling the hole. After seven or eight minutes, the hole was half-filled; the cement was very wet and had the consistency of quick sand. Luke peered down from his vantage point, and saw the concrete in the hole. He smiled and began to climb down; to check on the delivery, he made his way to the scaffolding. He was about to reach the platform; when from the side of him a figure appeared dressed in a long black, shiny coat, the hood was up and a scarf was covering the face, like a veil. The figure made a lunge at Luke; who jumped backwards, to avoid the figure's grasp and stumbled over one of the cross bars, attached to the scaffolding. The figure reached down and grabbed for Luke's sweatshirt, picking him up by it. The figure's strength was insurmountable as Luke tried to struggle. The figure moved Luke towards the side of the platform; it lifted him over the edge, still holding on to him. Suddenly the figure loosened its grasp and let him fall. Luke landed feet first, into the freshly poured concrete; the hole had been dug deep enough to support a two-storey structure, as he began to sink into the wet cement, the figure climbed down from the scaffolding.

"Hey! Come on this isn't fair man, what have I done to deserve this?" Luke asked.

He was trying to stay as still as he could to avoid sinking further, the figure moved across to the cement lorry. By then Luke had sunk down so far, only his head was showing; the figure moved the chute so that it was pointing over Luke's head. He watched as the figure put its hand into the coat pocket, it brought out a photograph and showed it to him. It was an old photo of Luke, Jez, Richard and Colin, taken twenty years back. He could see that Richard's face was crossed out, the figure turned the photo around, and on the other side he could read the words, **TARRED AND FEATHERED**. It then screwed up the photo and threw it at Luke hitting him in the face, then pulled out a Dictaphone and switched it on.

"Luke Jarvis, you are now being punished for your cruelty. You may have made a name for yourself as a builder all these years, but you've failed in your bid to become a decent human being. All the good things you've done up to this point, can't ever make up for the level of torment you forced upon one person,"

The Dictaphone clicked off again, Luke didn't have a chance to answer back, and the figure moved to release the lever on the cement lorry, allowing the cement to tumble out on to his face. The cement covered him completely, he coughed as it filled his mouth, and spat it back out. Because the force of the concrete was pressing down on him, totally covering his head, he couldn't breathe. The air ran out quickly and he suffocated, he was dead in moments and completely buried. Once the cement had emptied out, the figure switched off the lever, the pouring halted, and the chute was slid back into its holder. The figure then climbed back into the lorry, started the engine and drove slowly away from the house. Nobody had noticed the commotion in Luke's back garden; and the figure drove away inconspicuously.

Having given Luke's name as an alibi, Jez felt he should call round and warn him, that the police were on their way round, and they wanted to question him about where he'd been on Thursday morning. Jez knew he wasn't there, and also knew that the Cops wouldn't believe his story, if he told them he was with Steve's daughter Rita the night before. Steve's daughter kept her boyfriend a secret from him, because Steve's job meant he was naturally nosy about all things, including her love life. Jez and Rita had been secretly dating for the last six months, when Steve was at work they would see each other. Steve is protective of Rita; she is his only child and would challenge any man who pursued her favors. So, to respect Rita's wishes, Jez told Steve he was at Luke's house on Wednesday night. Jez got into his Ford Mondeo and waited for Steve and Paul to leave the station. He phoned Luke's mobile, but got an engaged tone, he threw his phone onto the passenger seat, started his car and proceeded to race the police, to get to Luke's house first. Steve and Paul had taken the long way around the estate, while Jez had raced along the main road at a colossal speed. Jez was getting to the bottom end of the main road, ready to turn into the Carmellen Estate. Just as he was approaching the turn he could see a large cement lorry coming towards him, on the other side of the road. Jez slowed his car to allow the lorry to pass, instead the lorry turned into his path and ploughed straight into Jez's car, head on. The impact pushed the Mondeo backwards up the road, and continued at speed, the cab was jammed on the front of the car, forcing it backwards, and still not reducing speed; Jez's car suddenly loosened and veered away from the lorry, shot backwards and hit the ditch at such a speed, it had catapulted up and somersaulted end over end into the field behind. The airbag had deployed, but because of the car somersaulting, it caused Jez's neck to snap back, breaking it with a sickening crunch. The car ceased rolling. His broken neck was fatal. Jez Stanley like his best friend Luke Jarvis had both been killed.

The lorry stopped further up the road and the figure driving it got out. It crossed the road to the field and went over to Jez's car where it lay on its roof. The occupants of the houses along that stretch of road, had heard the accident, and were looking out from their top floor windows to get a better look. The figure stared through the windscreen of Jez's car, quickly moved to check he was dead; then casually walked away, climbed back into the cement lorry, started the engine and drove away.

Meanwhile on the Carmellen estate, Steve and Paul had arrived outside Luke's house. Steve got out and walked up the recently renovated driveway. He continued to the front door of the house and rang the bell. There was no answer; then he rattled the doorknocker instead, hoping somebody would come to the door. The place was totally quiet, so Steve posted his calling card through the letterbox. Paul joined him, soon after.

"Nobody in then?" He asked.

"Let's go around the back, he might be working round there," Steve replied.

They walked around the side of Luke's house and into the back garden; they noticed the freshly laid cement, but didn't find anything else suspicious, it was beginning to set hard.

"It certainly doesn't look like he's here, Steve," said Paul. "Otherwise he'd have made the driver of that last load of concrete clean up after the pour, I've never seen such a mess."

"Probably he's been called out to help somebody with a problem," reasoned Steve.

They never even considered that Luke was buried alive by his own cement order, and left Luke's house without checking. Paul looked up and down the street, just to check if he could see Luke working anywhere else. He joined Steve again in his car, and they drove away, out of the bottom end of the estate. The driver's side window was wound down slightly; Steve could hear an Ambulance siren.

"Can you hear that?" Steve asked.

Paul cocked his ear to the window and listened.

"Let's get going then!" He ordered.

Steve floored his accelerator and sped quickly away up the road. They drove out of the estate to the main road, turned right and as they drove along a couple of hundred metres, they could see the wreckage of a purple Mondeo and slowed down to take control of the situation.

"Holy cow; what a mess!" Steve said with astonishment.

Steve and Paul took over the scene, they had got out of the car and began recording a few details; the road had parts of Jez's car all the way along it. The scene they were looking at was one of utter carnage. Steve had traffic cones in the back of his car and carried them out, sealing off the scene at either end of that section of road. Paul carried some rods along and put them into the traffic cones, and then Steve weaved yellow incident tape through the rods.

"This road needs to remain sealed off until the wreck can be towed away, and this shit on the road cleared away," said Paul, assuming command of the situation.

He phoned the station to report the crash, and he requested more materials to be brought down, then he could divert traffic away from the scene. The ambulance raced along, siren still sounding. Paul waved them over to the crash-sight. They could see one man's body, just showing out of the driver's side door. Steve couldn't make out who it was from his position, although the car looked familiar. Paul strolled purposefully along the main road; he was measuring the distance from where the glass first lay on the road, to the large gap in the hedge where the car had gone through. He crossed the road and took out a small digital camera, and began taking pictures of the scene. The paramedics were gathering their apparatus out of the ambulance; they rushed to the wreck, one paramedic was phoning for a fire engine, so that the petrol spill could be made safe. While they were waiting, Steve was pacing up and down; he wanted to go over and get a closer look at the victim and wondered whether he knew him.

Paul noticed that the residents on the road were looking over at the accident and tapped Steve on the shoulder and said.

"I'm going to speak to them, and see if I can get some answers."

Steve nodded and Paul walked away to the first group of people. The response from the Fire Service was excellent, they reached the scene within five minutes, the car was sprayed with foam, and the Paramedics began with their rescue. Steve watched this take place and couldn't believe it was all happening, three terrible incidents since Saturday. A normal week would be one or two car thefts, a touch of vandalism, maybe a chase or two, after stolen cars. This was beginning to concern Steve, nothing on this scale has ever happened here before, and he'd been living there for fifteen years. When he worked in the City, he had only been involved in one murder case, and a couple of domestic violence issues. This was a whole new ball game, even Paul was surprised by it all, he's been living here longer, and secretly hoped that it wouldn't get any busier than this. Steve thought maybe Paul was right and bad luck was starting to happen, he cursed to himself and paid him the £50 they had wagered earlier. Paul could only say,

"I wish I'd never noticed those bloody blackbirds."

They began their investigations.

Chapter 6

Clueless Blues

Paul Collison started to interview the small crowd that was appearing, as if by magic out of the houses to get information about the accident, while he was doing that, Steve was checking over the crash site. Two of the ambulance crew were crouched over the body; they managed to get him from the car and on to a stretcher. Steve went over and looked with disbelief and put his hands to his brow.

"This is Jeremy Stanley, we only just spoken to him this afternoon, what's he doing down here?"

"Don't know Detective, we got the call about twenty minutes ago," the Paramedic replied.

"Is he dead?" Steve then asked.

"Yes; almost certainly instantaneous, from a broken neck, but the pathologist should confirm all that."

"Take him straight to the mortuary, I'll call Shabby," Steve ordered.

The paramedics loaded the stretcher into the back of the ambulance, with Jez's body on it. They began packing away their equipment, got in and drove away quietly with no siren or lights. Steve realized now that his questioning earlier at the station, was irrelevant. Jeremy was extremely unlikely to have been the murderer, if he was dead himself, and genuinely did find Richard's body, just like he had said.

Paul Collison had finished gathering his information and joined Steve back at the wrecked car.

"The residents that witnessed the crash saw a cement lorry pushing the Mondeo backwards up the road," said Paul, pointing and making a motion from where the first resident's observation was made to where the Mondeo ended up. "A couple of the residents got a look at the lorry driver, you won't believe this either, it is the same description as the first case, a tall person, wearing a long black shiny coat, the hood over its head. They say it got out of the lorry briefly to look at the crashed car, and then drove off," Paul added.

"The crash happened on purpose, didn't it?" Steve asked.

"Looks like it Steve," Paul replied.

Steve began checking the damage of the car; he looked back up the road, which Paul had pointed out; there was glass on the road, about one hundred metres back, this must have been the impact point; he couldn't see any skid marks.

"Jeremy didn't have any time to brake, the lorry driver had crossed on to his side, he had no chance of surviving this, a cast iron case of hit and run," Steve pointed out.

"I'll give my mate Graeme from traffic a call, he can come down and examine all this," Paul said.

"Yeah, give him a call, have him check where that cement lorry came from, and I'll go around to Jeremy's family, they'll need to know what happened here, they've got to formally identify him anyway," Steve replied.

Paul called his mate on his mobile and Steve returned to his car, he knew yet again, that he had to drive to the Carmellen Estate, and give more bad news to parents, who had just lost their kid. While Steve was driving, he started to practise in his head, what he was going to say to the Stanleys. He knew them well; they live across the road from him, they are a very close family. Jeff Stanley was always posing with his ride-on lawnmower; driving around his front lawn in fast, the whole family were show offs. Jeff had his own successful business making furniture in the workshop behind the house. His wife Helen worked at the school teaching history and sociology. Jez's sister, Jordanna, is a pretty girl only twenty-one, much younger than Jez, an aspiring gymnast, who regularly won competitions, when she was younger. Jeff was one of those men who exuded confidence, so Steve had a small laugh to himself when he remembered the time Jez had ridden the lawnmower, and crashed it into Jeff's pride and joy, his silver Bentley. Than he realized that Jez won't be performing stunts like that anymore, and quickly changed his mood to focus on his job. He turned left and around the corner, pulled up about fifty yards, and waited outside the Stanley household. He could see his house and his wife was in the front garden, she hadn't noticed Steve had stopped by. He whistled at her, with a shrill tone, she looked up and smiled at him, he trotted over the road to her.

"I've got to deliver bad news to the Stanleys; I'll be over later,"

She waved at him in her usual dismissive way, as he walked up the driveway of the Stanleys. His knock on the door was met by a huge bark from the family dog, a Chocolate Doberman.

"Zane! Get back, turnip," was Jeff's response to the dogs barking.

The dog scuttled away on command and Jeff opened the door, he was surprised to see Steve standing there.

"Hello Steve, what's my boy done now?" Jeff jokingly asked.

"I need to come in Jeff," said Steve in a glum tone. "Are your wife and daughter here?" He inquired.

"Yes, they are, come on in then," said Jeff obediently. "Helen! Jordanna! Come to the family room, will you?" Jeff called, in the same commanding voice as he had just delivered to the dog.

The men waited in the lounge for the women to come in. First Jordanna entered, she smiled shyly and sat on the floor in front of the T.V, the dog approached her protectively and sat on his haunches beside her, Zane looked at Steve instantly knowing his news, and gave a whine, and Jordanna patted him on the back. A few seconds later Helen came in, wiping her hands on a tea towel, she stood with Jeff for a moment and then lit a cigarette.

"I came to tell you in person, because you are my neighbors, that Jeremy has been involved in a traffic accident. The crash was fatal, he has broken his neck, and unfortunately he died from his injuries at the scene," Steve informed them.

Gasps and instant crying met his news.

"What happened then?" Asked Jeff, with an air of complete shock.

Helen had moved to Jordanna and they stood holding each other, both sobbing, Zane just circled them, again protecting them.

"We believe it may be a hit and run Jeff, the locals say it was a large lorry, it hit him head on, it could have been deliberate," was Steve's answer.

"The medics have taken him to the mortuary; we will need you to formally identify him,"

Jeff nodded then went to comfort Helen and Jordanna; Steve gave Zane a quick pat, turned to the Stanley family and said,

"Do any of you have a spare key to Jez's flat please?" Steve asked.

"Yeah, just a second," said Jeff, and he went over to his key shelf in the hall; picked up a key and then walked back to Steve, Jeff handed it to him. "What do you need it for?" Jeff inquired.

"I just wanted to have a look around, check to see if there are any clues, if it was deliberate, maybe I'll find something," Steve replied. "I am sorry to come here and be the bearer of bad news; but we will get to the bottom if this, that's a promise," he added.

He wasn't convincing himself, about fulfilling this promise at that moment in time.

"Yeah, I know what you mean Detective, the Jones twins, Richard and now Jeremy. They're all dead within a fortnight, when will it end?" Jeff asked.

"I can't answer that right now Jeff, we will endeavour to solve this quickly as we can," Steve assured him. With that note he made his exit, Jeff followed Steve out, the women were still very upset about the news.

"I'm sorry Jeff, he was a terrific boy, this is going to be tough for you, if you feel like a beer or just to talk, then call over," offered Steve.

"We'll be at the mortuary this evening, if that is okay? It will take a while to call the family and tell them the news," explained Jeff.

"Take your time," replied Steve, then turned around and walked down the road, leaving his car where it was and trudged across to his house. He took out his mobile, called the station and told them he was having an extended dinner break. Inside his house, Steve went to find his wife, she was sat at the breakfast bar reading a recipe book in the kitchen.

"Bren, Jeremy from over the road was killed earlier, he was involved in a hit and run," said Steve.

She put the book down and gave Steve a long cuddle; this surprised him, she would hardly touch him these days.

"You had better tell Rita, dear," she said, with authority. "Jeremy and Rita were close, she'll be upset by this, so tell her soon as you can," she ordered.

Steve looked confused; he hadn't noticed this before, how it was that he was kept out of the loop like this?

"You mean they were seeing each other, why didn't you tell me this?" He demanded.

"Rita didn't tell anyone, I guessed they were a couple, she left her mobile phone behind once, I read one of the text messages, it isn't rocket science to know when your daughter is happy and in love with someone," she pointed out.

Steve felt foolish, he hadn't even noticed, now these attacks on people were beginning to get personal, he reasoned that it wouldn't be long before his daughter might be a target. His over protectiveness kicked in, and he immediately went to phone her. The receptionist at Rita's office patched the call through to her. She worked in the City as a financial advisor, she was brilliant with numbers, she supervised an office of eight juniors, and her bosses were generous enough to leave her working alone, using her own skills and devices to run it as she pleased. The girl on reception spoke with a high squeaky voice.

"Miss Speed, your dad is on the line, says it's urgent," the girl said.

"Thanks Clare, I'll take it from here," Rita replied.

"Dad, how are you, what's wrong?" She asked with surprise.

"You should try and finish work early today love, come over to our house please, we've got some bad news," he ordered.

"If it's bad news, I'll come now, give me an hour, and I'll be there," she said readily.

Steve finished his phone call and made a quick snack to eat, polished it off with ravenous ease, as he hadn't eaten properly for two days. Brenda returned to the kitchen, and started to prepare the recipe she had read earlier, while they were there together, Steve noticed his wife, probably for the first time in a couple of years, how beautiful and accomplished she was, in everything she did. Feeding him meals, looking after the house, her job at the hospital, noticing how perplexed he was with this case, taking care of their daughter's issues. He realized how lucky he was and hadn't even noticed lately. He promised himself, that he would dedicate more time to them in the future. The next hour went by very quickly, Rita was steering her car into the drive. When she came into the house, she went straight to her father.

"Why is your car outside Jeremy's parent's house?" Rita asked.

"That is what we wanted you to come over for Love, don't worry you're not in trouble for going out with him or anything," Steve said calmly.

She felt a little embarrassed that her dad knew, but to her relief was glad he was cool about it. Rita went into the kitchen, kissed her mother hello, and she sat with her at the breakfast bar.

"What is the bad news then Dad, why have I come all the way over?" She asked.

"Jeremy spoke to us earlier this morning, he found his cousin in the woods, and he'd been shot dead "

She gasped when he told her and looked at her mother for a moment. She couldn't believe what her dad had just told her, Brenda just blinked sadly and Rita knew there was more news to follow.

"We questioned him about the killing at the station, he gave us Luke Jarvis as an alibi, so we went to check it out, while we were doing that, he was driving another way round to the estate. On the way, a lorry had hit him, his car was sent flying back and into a field, the impact made him break his neck and well, to be blunt, he's dead," explained Steve.

Rita's mouth contorted with shock and she flung herself into her mother's arms and began to cry.

"I've told the Stanley family, and they are devastated by the news," he continued. "I didn't realize you were together until this evening, we suspect that Jeremy was killed on purpose, just like Richard. The killer seems to be going around and targeting these people for some reason. I am worried now that perhaps, you've become a target, so I am asking you to be careful and when you've had time to speak to the Stanleys, stay in the City until this loony is caught; promise me?" He pleaded.

Rita nodded, her tears stained her mother's top, and Steve joined in with the embrace and kissed Rita's forehead.

"I have to go back to work now and see if I can solve this shambles, the pressure is on us to get a result, before the Regional Serious Crime Squad come down here and bully us," said Steve. "Bren; this could take a couple of days I'm afraid. Rita; try not to worry, go and see the Stanleys, they'll be glad of the company," instructed Steve.

"I'll go with her, darling," said Brenda.

With that he kissed them both, left the house and returned to work.

His first port of call was Jez's flat; he arrived outside the block of flats that Jez lived in; the same kids he met last week were there again, except they didn't say anything this time. He walked to the door and buzzed the intercom; the door was locked after seven o'clock at night. The warden answered the buzzer.

"Who is it?"

"I'm Detective Steve Speed, Mortal Dean Police and I have come to have a look around Jeremy Stanley's flat," Steve answered; he flashed his warrant card at the C.C.T.V camera.

"Right, wait a moment," the warden called back, he pressed the buzzer, allowing the door to open.

Steve walked up to level two; the flat number on the key was 203. He went to the correct numbered door, opened it and went inside, closed the front door behind him and approached the sitting room, once inside his eyes scanned around. Jez's flat was typical for a man of his nature, a real bachelor's pad. Plasma T.V, black ash furniture, stylish and colour coded with the rug and curtains. On the bookcase was a large photograph of Jez, Jordanna, Richard and Cathy, framed in silver; he noticed how happy they all looked. Next to this was a key ring with a photo hanging from it; it was of Jez and Rita. Steve realized how loving they looked, their cheeks pressed together and grinning. He left the key ring there, and hadn't picked it up. He continued his inspection, and methodically searched the whole flat. He noticed a pile of gun magazines on the coffee table, and a couple of car ones too. He picked up the gun magazine at the top, as it fell open, an old polaroid dropped out. This made Steve screw his face up, it was of the missing Gerard Swales and he looked in a bad way, his hands looked tied behind him and he'd been crying. He put this picture in his jacket pocket. His search continued, he looked in the kitchen but found nothing of note. He quickly concluded that Jez hasn't been home for a couple of days; maybe he spent some time with Rita. Steve began to realize how serious they were as a couple, this made him worry for his daughter's safety. He finished his search and then left the flat for the police station. Back at the station, Paul Collison had just finished his report about the car accident; he had put a photo of Jeremy on the incident board, now there were four photos up. He had written short notes in black letters next to each of the victims. There was Betty and Caitlin's photo, happy and smiling, under that a photo of their charred remains, he had written **BURNT BEYOND RECOGNITION, WHY?** Next to Richard's photo again smiling, supplied by Cathy, and underneath this, one with his horrific injuries, Paul had written **EXPERTLY EXECUTED, WHY?** He was beginning to write the piece for Jeremy, when Steve came into the room looking shattered.

"Don't put anything up there yet, we don't know why he's been sought out," Steve suggested.

"Fair enough, Steve," said Paul, and in the middle of these photos, wrote next to the artist's impression of the killer, **WHY ARE YOU DOING THIS?**

"That is a good question Paul, one I would like answers from very quickly, pal," Steve insisted, as he went to his desk and slumped into his chair, his fingers were pressed into his forehead, and his thoughts were pensive and deliberate.

"That Jeremy Stanley was seeing Rita, she said he's been with her for six months, and I didn't even notice," He explained.

"I can see why you are thinking deeply, you're anxious and you want this solved quickly, in case Rita becomes a target," said Paul.

Steve nodded at his concerns; he snatched up his phone to call Shabby. When the call came to Shabby's office, he was scrutinizing Richard's remains for a final time. Next to Richard laid Jez, he had just been wheeled in. The bruising around his neck was dark black. His assistant handed him the receiver, he took it with his left hand, and with tweezers in his right hand, was folding back pieces of skin on Richard's face, and removing shotgun pellets.

"Shabby, its Steve here, there's been another death, this time hit and run, same killer or killers, just a different mode of death," Steve explained.

Shabby stared at Jez for a moment.

"Aye, I can see, that makes four altogether, can you make any connections at all?" Shabby inquired.

"This one is Jeremy Stanley, he is a cousin of the victim you are currently examining, and he has a broken neck, quick death this time. What's more, he was the boyfriend of my daughter Rita," Steve replied.

Shabby could see the toe label tied to Jez.

"The twins were best friends with Mr Joiner, so yeah; they're beginning to connect in some way. We just don't know why he's doing it," Steve went on to explain.

"The killer clearly didn't want him to talk to anyone, makes me think that he was watching these victims, before making his move," reasoned Shabby.

"Then this maniac knows Jeremy was seeing Rita, which makes it even more imperative that we protect her. I will speak to some of my pals over in the Met, to keep an eye on her when she goes back to work," said Steve, ending his conversation.

Shabby put down the phone and continued his work; Steve walked over to his incident board, he wrote on it next to Jeremy's photo, **WHO DIDN'T THE KILLER WANT YOU TO TALK TO AND WHY?** He put his hand in his jacket pocket, and pulled out the photo of Gerard, found in Jez's flat, and he gazed at it for a moment, he couldn't understand why the kid looked so sad, but he was going to find out, and he put it away inside his desk drawer.

The time was pressing on; it was nearly eleven o'clock at night. He sat for a while and formulated a plan, which victim would this lunatic go for next. Which method would it choose, the last couple of events took place in a sequence of thirty-six hours, and the last one was at three o'clock earlier that afternoon. Steve thought that he would go on a drive around Mortal Dean at about four o'clock in the morning, he thought maybe he would uncover something suspicious going on, catch the killer in the act perhaps. The time came around for him to go; he went to his car and began driving, parking up at regular intervals, to catch any strange activities. Steve knew with a gut instinct that soon the killer would strike again and that instinct was from being a copper, nothing to do with any blackbirds.

Chapter 7

Chicken Factory Trials

At the north end of Mortal Dean, on the outskirts of the village, sits Sirtes Poultry Supplies, which is a chicken-processing factory and the company employs over one hundred people on shift-work. The shifts run from ten o'clock at night, to six o'clock in the morning, from six o'clock in the morning, to two o'clock in the afternoon, and from two o'clock up to ten o'clock at night, all three shifts were allocated a quota of chickens per shift. There is always a government inspector who insists that the birds are treated humanely, and a veterinarian in attendance at all times. Most of the chickens came from Brown Gale farm; the Swales family ran a battery of chickens for eggs, and have plenty of land for thousands of free-range hens and cocks for mass breeding purposes. The business was profitable for the Swales, the birds served them well, with meat, eggs and even fertilizer were all produced from them. Gregg took these chickens still alive to the factory, every night. Georgina ran the breeding side of the business; they had taken over from their father when he retired. Their mother still held a vested interest, just to steer her children in the right direction, in case there were snags. The shifts at the factory split teams into three crews. Crew one would kill the chickens and they came down a chute to the production line, and there were five of these, two people stood at each side. This crew would pick them up and after being stunned with an electric probe, slit their throats. They would place them on hooks by their feet to ride through to crew two; they would pluck the feathers, behead them, remove their gizzards and chop off the feet. They were then conveyed to Colin Rusdale; shift leader and his butcher's crew. In his schooldays, Colin had been the force behind the gang that tormented Gerard. He led a team of ten; they would fillet, half or quarter the chickens as required, and then the wings, legs and breasts, were packaged separately. In Colin's team were Zach Dagan, Stuart Warner, Phil Barker and Sean Curle, plus the five packers, Cyril, Kevin, David, Walter and Percy, who were in a different part of the factory from the butchers, working in the loading bay.

The four o'clock whistle sounded and every one stopped for a fifteen-minute tea break. There was a buzz of workers as Colin led his team to the loading bay, where they could go outside and have a smoke with the shutters raised. Everybody else had gone to the canteen for teas and coffees. Colin stood by the loading doors breathing in the fresh air, while his team finished their cigarettes. He had his own bottle of drink; he was an asthmatic and his bosses allowed him to carry water with him. He took a good gulp from the bottle and turned to his team.

"Finish your fags and get back to it boys, okay?" Colin ordered.

They hurriedly lit another cigarette each, and Colin disappeared back through the factory doors. The other men finished their breaks and returned to work, they were all in position, ready for the production line, and then suddenly there was a power cut. They were stood in darkness, blinking into the black.

"This is going to shit up production," Colin remarked.

"Hey! What the hell's going on?" Some of the men shouted together.

"Don't worry, I'll go to the plant room and have a look at the fuse box," said Colin.

He knew the factory well, even in the darkness; he followed the luminous green line along the floor. Zach and Stuart went with him, when they reached the plant room Colin opened the door then stepped inside. Zach and Stuart waited outside while he checked the fuses.

"The switches are all on, the power must be cut from the source or something," suggested Colin.

He went to step out of the room, but somebody had grabbed him from behind, whoever it was, had their arm around Colin's neck and his left arm folded up his back.

"Sssh! Don't say anything or I'll break it," a calm disembodied voice said, referring to his arm, it was tugged upwards to prove a point.

Colin felt the pain, but didn't make a sound, the person holding him pushed the door closed, and locked it. The room was completely black, but the figure could see Colin, as it had on night vision glasses. His captor let him go, and flung him to the ground, they were still in the dark, so Colin couldn't make out who it was.

"While you lay there, why don't we reflect on a few things from the past shall we?" The voice requested.

Colin couldn't quite place the voice; it was distorted in some way. He tried to see through the pitch black and noticed a glint of something metal, it flashed before his eyes. From outside the door, frantic banging could be heard; Zach and Stuart were trying to break in. With that noise going on outside, the killer knew it had plenty of time, the voice continued its trip down memory lane.

"Take a moment to think back, you were the ring leader of a gang of boys, twenty-five years ago, try and remember Colin, this is important. At school, you led around, Ricky, Jez and Luke. For those five years, they were good friends of yours, and during that time between you, made one person's life a living nightmare," the voice explained.

Suddenly Colin remembered Gerard, thoughts flashed through his mind, all the things he had done to him.

"Look, some of those things weren't my idea, Richard and Jez thought most of them up, he really wound them up," pleaded Colin.

"Don't blame them, they're already taken care of, you are the last of the group," said the voice.

"What do you mean, taken care of?"

"Didn't you get the gossip, Colin? Richard and Jez are dead, the police have found them, but they haven't found Luke yet, and you're not going to tell either, 'cause it's your turn now."

"Oh no, please, I didn't know, I've just got back from holiday, this is my first shift back," begged Colin.

He stood up, his nerves getting the better of him, but as he stood there, he felt something sharp slice his throat. Blood began spraying out, and he put his hands over the wound to stop the flow, but it just carried on spurting. Colin was gurgling and spluttering, trying to stay conscious, he dropped to the floor; his life was being drained from him. A few more seconds and Colin lay dead at the feet of his killer, who undid the lock and flung the door wide open; as it knew Zach and Stuart were there on the other side. Street lighting from outside the factory lit the room these two men were standing in. The killer stepped backwards, there was a noisy commotion coming from the factory, voices of men were calling and panicking. This provided cover for the killer's next move, in one hand it held a knife, but in the other hand it was holding a fire axe from the plant room, the killer stepped out from the darkened room, and rushed at Stuart, who had moved back from the door, after it had been unlocked. Zach had moved to behind a table next to the door. The killer swung the axe at Stuart, who'd leaned back from the swing, but he banged his head on the wall, this made him move forward, and the axe's blade hit him hard, right in the centre of his chest, the killer pulled it out with force, making Stuart fall forward, he just lay there, and blood was flowing from the wound on to the floor. Zach made his move, but got an elbow in the face for his trouble, this made him fall back, the killer held on to him as he fell and stabbed at Zach four times, plunging the knife deeply into his body. Zach and Stuart lay together on the floor, both bleeding badly. The killer stood for a few seconds, looking at them both.

"Sorry men, I'm not angry with you two, it's not your fault, you are just sheep for this man, you were in the wrong place at the wrong time," said the voice.

It left them there, and escaped through a fire exit, twenty metres away. Stuart died where he was lying, but Zach was still clinging to his life, he crawled on his stomach to the plant room, where Colin was. Suddenly the lights came back on, and all the machinery started whirring into use. Zach could see Colin, his jugular vein had been severed, blood was all over him, and he was lying on his back. Zach stopped crawling and stayed still, but he didn't last much longer either, the knife had cut him fatally, four times into his lungs at different places. It all suddenly went cold for him and he drifted quietly away. The rest of the team realized that Colin, Zach and Stuart were missing; Phil knew something was wrong, so he went to find them, and Phil led the way with Sean following.

"Split up and start searching the factory, something's wrong, go in groups and shout if you find anything," Phil commanded.

Cyril took Kevin with him and Walter, David and Percy went another way. They searched the entire factory, recruiting the rest of the shift workers, in the process. The production process had completely halted; everyone was looking for the missing men.

"Arrgh! In here guys," yelled Sean, after finding Stuart.

Phil then found Colin and Zach further over.

"Some bastard's really done a number on them, the blackout wasn't an accident," said Phil, trying to control his emotions.

"Don't bloody touch anything," Sean said.

By this time there were some twenty-five men and women, all looking and gasping with shock at the scene.

"You don't think the killer is still here do you?" Cyril asked.

Phil shrugged; he began calling the emergency services.

"Call the governors, tell them not to send in the next two shifts today, in fact, they'll have to close the factory for a while," Phil ordered.

Sean went to call the factory owners; he ran up the stairs quickly to the offices, he didn't want to be the killer's next victim. Sean was in the office looking for the telephone numbers, out of the corner of his eye, he noticed movement from outside the factory, he turned to look out the window, and saw it was a figure looking up at him; it was standing with its hands in the pockets, of the long black coat it was wearing. The figure motioned to Sean; it made a slit across the throat gesture and then moved off up the road, it was running very quickly away. Seeing this made Sean very nervous, but he continued with his task of calling the factory owners...

It was six o'clock in the morning and Steve was driving along one of the main roads, it was the long road heading south out of Mortal Dean, his car phone began to ring. Steve pulled the car over to take the call; when he answered, it was Paul Collison.

"Steve, where are you? I've been trying to get you for about half an hour."

"I must have dozed off for a bit Paul; I've been out here in Mortal Dean all night."

"Well! Get your arse over to Sirtes Chicken Factory, there's been more deaths Steve."

"Right Paul, on my way, did you call Shabby?"

"He's on his way over too, he'll meet you there," Paul answered. "I'm bringing over several uniform, they'll be needed for the questioning of the witnesses."

Paul broke off the call and Steve turned his car, one hundred and eighty degrees around, and drove to the factory. He breathed a sigh of relief, he realized that Rita wasn't the killers next target. He still felt uncomfortable that it had struck again, and while he was out and about, supposedly looking for it. The killer was beginning to make Steve look foolish, this made him feel angry, and he floored his accelerator to get to the factory. Eventually Steve arrived at the factory, Shabby's car was there, and Paul Collison was standing at the back doors of a police van, giving out last minute instructions to his fellow officers. Steve walked over to Shabby; who was waiting for him, he was stroking his chin.

"I bet you are secretly relieved it isn't your daughter," said Shabby.

"Still should solve this one though Shabs, what have we got this time?"

"Three, all of them male, all the same age, thirty-six, it's a real blood bath this time, this is the man who called us, Mr Barker," said Collison.

He had been waiting for the police to arrive, and his face was pale with shock, he had smoked about four cigarettes in that time.

"All the workers are gathered in the staff canteen, nobody's touched anything, the owners have been called, and they are on their way here, they'll be a while, as they live in the City," Phil explained.

"Thanks Mr Barker, please lead the way," said Shabby, moving his hand to guide Phil in front of him.

They all walked with Phil down the main production area, the uniformed police entered the canteen, and they clustered around, beginning to talk with the factory workers, trying to get information. Steve, Shabby and Paul continued on, to the scene in the power room.

"Right, here it is then officers, I'll go back to the canteen, now that you're here."

All three officers put on their latex gloves; Shabby went to Colin's body first. Steve stood over Stuart and looked at the gaping hole in his chest. Paul had positioned himself next to Zach's body, kneeling.

"Why three this time, and they all have cutting injuries, is this significant?" Shabby questioned his Dictaphone. He clicked off the machine and looked at Steve, and he was waiting to hear a remark.

"They are all wearing aprons, and those silly shower hats, this suggests they're the butchers of this operation, that may be the connection," Steve theorized.

"I don't think these two were his target out here, I believe they were a bonus, maybe he was disturbed by these two," suggested Shabby.

"Mr Barker says there was a power cut, it lasted for about an hour, shortly after it came back on these guys were found," Paul chipped in.

"I reckon the killer cut the power, lay in wait for this guy, because it was dark, didn't see these two out here, I also think this man was locked in and then killed, look there's a bloody hand mark on the handle and lock. The killer was messy this time, but still efficient enough to end their lives," Shabby pointed out.

"So, he had to kill the other two, just in case they squealed," said Steve.

Shabby, studied Colin's wound.

"A straight slice across the throat," he noted on his Dictaphone, as he moved to Stuart and looked at his wound.

"One fatal blow to the chest, very easy," he said. Lastly Shabby went to Zach. "This one has four stab wounds, makes me think he tried to fight him, same outcome though, killed easily," he concluded.

"This killer is getting more confident with each kill, and furthermore he is enjoying leaving nothing behind, for us to find, where are the murder weapons?" Steve added.

Shabby clicked off his Dictaphone again, after hearing Steve's remark; he turned his head to look down the corridor, bloody footprints led to the fire exit.

"Well at least he left something, these have a sole tread on it look, a pair of Wellington boots. They look like the same boots as the other workers, means he was probably here before the power cut. These boots won't be hard to find and we will look for these, when we investigate further," said Shabby, pointing at the footprints, and crouching down to see more easily. "The injuries to this first man one slice across the throat by a hunting knife; with a very sharp blade. This man was hit with a fire axe, look there's one missing," hinted Shabby, pointing to the empty space on the plant room wall. "And the third man was attacked with the same type of knife as the first victim."

"Well he must have taken them with him, because they aren't here, are they?" Steve pointed out.

Shabby had finished his part of the investigation, photographing the scene and calling the Coroner. Steve and Paul were making their final notes and wrapping up also. Paul led the two men back to the canteen; they came down the corridor and were met by a uniformed officer, escorting Sean.

"This gentleman is Mr Curle; says he saw something, from the window of the office," said the officer. "Well go on, tell the Sergeant?"

"I was making a call to the factory owners, and saw a person stood outside, it was looking at me and made a threatening gesture, like my throat was going to be cut or something," explained Sean.

Paul put this in his notes.

"And what happened then?"

"Nothing, I was scared for a bit, but it just sprinted up the road, after that."

"What was this person wearing, or did you see a face?" Paul inquired.

"No I didn't see a face, it was covered with something, like a scarf, it wore a coat, a very long one, it looked kind of shiny, the hood was up," Sean explained.

"Yeah okay, I get it, same killer," said Steve, who was listening.

"Thanks, Mr Curle, you've been very helpful," said Paul, as they walked away to the car park.

"That man may be the killer's next target, we'll have to keep him under observation," suggested Shabby.

Steve and Paul nodded to each other; they made that a priority. Shabby stayed back to wait for the Coroner; he began to smoke a cigarette, and puffed impatiently, while he waited. Meanwhile Steve waited for Sean to leave work. This was one time where he wished he still smoked, but his craving was short lived. He returned to his car and waited. Steve couldn't get what he had seen at the factory out of his mind. Whoever the killer was, it wasn't the usual run of the mill psychopath, and it was much more clinical and precise than that, like the person had studied anatomy or something similar, and who knew where all the kill spots were on a human body. Hard as this case is to crack, Steve was determined to solve it and soon.

Sean drove out of the factory and turned left to what Steve thought would be home, instead a couple of hundred metres from the factory, he suddenly pulled into a driveway of another house, Steve passed him so as not to alert his pursuant, and pulled over a few more metres away. Sean got out of his car and walked to the front door of the house. He knocked and a woman answered, she seemed to know Sean well, because she was kissing him at length on the doorstep. Steve didn't really want to hang around while these two played tonsil hockey, so he began to turn his car around and leave. Sean and the woman disappeared into the house, by the shadow at the front door; they were already tearing the clothes off each other. Steve realized that Sean was in for the time of his life, and he didn't really enjoy what he was witnessing. It was seven AM by this time, so Steve sloped off for some breakfast at his own house. He thought Sean and the lucky lady, would be at least two hours, and he would begin his stake out of Sean after. Inside his own place, Steve crept about quietly, Brenda had been working nights at the hospital, and she would have his nuts in a sling, if he woke her right now. He took out bread from the pantry and buttered it; and some cold bacon, he made a sandwich, and he poured orange juice into a glass and gulped it down fast. He ate his sandwich greedily and sat waiting for the two hours to pass. Then he would begin his surveillance properly, on a full stomach. The two hours passed quickly and Steve was raring to go again.

❈

Chapter 8

The Morgue is Filling Up

Steve followed Sean to his house and watched him go in, he pulled his car over and waited for him to come back out. Sitting there at the side of the road gave him the chance of going over recent events in his head. So far there are seven people killed by one person, what would make someone like that get so crazy that they would end the lives of these individuals? He knew that, five of them were killed on purpose, but two were probably just taken out for being in the way. This made the killer very unpredictable and unstable, this time the killer had been careless and left a lot of mess, or was that done on purpose too. The whole thing was confusing; Shabby seemed to have the case by the balls and was making progress, but Steve was still none the wiser. Then suddenly a thought came into Steve's head, maybe Shabby was the killer, he knew the murder weapons, he knew how they were killed and he was waiting at the scene before everyone else. These thoughts were a bit irrational, but to him it all made some sort of sense, but one thing Shabby didn't know, was the victim's names. Steve thought he should keep an open mind about Shabby from now on, he knew how clever he could be, and Steve didn't like being made a fool of. Just then, Sean reappeared at his front door, he'd changed his clothes and looked clean, he went to his car and started it up, Steve followed suit, Sean pulled away from the house and Steve tailed him.

Back at the mortuary, Shabby had taken delivery of last night's killings and, before starting on them, was finalising the paperwork allowing Richard and Jez's bodies to be released for their final certification. He and his assistant signed the forms and handed the bodies back to the Coroner's office, which were waiting to take them away.

"Please call Mr and Mrs Joiner, and Mr and Mrs Stanley. They can at last say goodbye to their sons," Shabby said to Sara.

She nodded quietly and began to telephone the families. Shabby made his way back to the labs, and dressed in his gown and mask, ready to examine the next three victims. He knew these would be quick autopsies, compared to the other four he had performed; he had time to prepare some notes from the previous examinations. He'd begun writing when the phone rang, he answered it, and the caller was Paul Collison.

"Shabby, my mate Graeme from traffic called me, apparently, they've recovered a mobile phone, from the Mondeo Mr Stanley was driving, and they have put it in as evidence."

"Have them sent over to my office would you Paul?"

"It's on the way over to you now," replied Paul. He hung up and returned to his duties. Shabby continued with his paperwork, his assistant appeared next to him with a sheet of paper, and she placed it in front of him.

"The two weapons from the Joiner case were bought at the same place, and on the same day, Guns and Ammo Ltd, suppliers of weapons in the City," she said and pointed out the description of the shopper at the bottom of the paragraph. "A woman in her late forties, and she paid by credit card."

"Get someone up there for a statement and ask for a copy of the receipt please Sara?" She nodded her head and promptly disappeared again.

Back at Mortal Dean police station, Paul Collison was writing his reports from this mornings' goings on, Simon came to his desk, he put a piece of note paper into Paul's hand.

"This woman, Mrs Froggat; says she had arranged for Mr Jarvis to go to her house and finish off her electrical wiring, she'd paid him in advance for the work, she's tried both his home and his mobile with no success and with all this stuff about murders on the news, thought she ought to report it," Simon explained. "I've had some work done by this Luke Jarvis, he's pretty good at his job, when he agrees to a contract he always turns up, he's as reliable as your wristwatch."

"Right, I'll go around later and speak to her, thanks Simon," said Paul, and he continued with his report.

Meanwhile back at the Carmellen estate, Sean had stopped in the road to speak to Phil; Steve hung back in his car to see what would happen next. The pair of them looked tired and nervous, Sean was looking around all the time, but he didn't notice Steve sitting in his car behind, by the looks of things Sean was telling Phil about who he had seen earlier that morning, Phil's face was as pale as Sean's top, the men then parked their cars up at the local shops and walked across the road to the Tug Boat Inn. Steve realized he couldn't wait out here all afternoon, so he left them to it and returned to the police station.

In the Stanley household, the telephone rang; it was the Coroner's office, Jeff had taken the call.

"This is Karl Lawstone, I'm the Coroner, the bodies of Richard and Jeremy have been released to us, and you may now come and visit."

"Thanks Mr Lawstone, we will instruct you accordingly, please allow me time to call the family, and we will be in touch," said Jeff.

"Certainly, Mr Stanley, please keep us informed."

Jeff put the phone down, and he called Helen and Jordanna.

"Hey girls, there's some news, we can go and see Ricky and Jeremy," said Jeff. "The Coroner has finished his reports, give Cathy a call, she'll be pleased."

Helen and Jordanna hugged each other when they heard the news; Helen used the kitchen phone to call Cathy. The phone rang at Cathy's house; she had been drinking heavily, since Richard's death. She looked unwashed with two-day-old make-up still on her face, her hair was matted, and she had really let herself go. She slowly staggered over to the phone, holding her glass of gin in her left hand, and nearly spilling it with careless abandon; she slurped at it and then answered the telephone.

"Who is it?" Cathy slurred. "It can't be Ricky, because he's dead."

"No dear, it's Auntie Helen, we've heard from the Coroner, we can now say goodbye to the boys properly."

Cathy drank again from the gin, and this time the glass dropped to the floor, breaking as it landed.

"Oh goody, first my best friends, now my boyfriend and his cousin, who will we have to bury next?" Cathy questioned.

"Hopefully that is all the people from our family; thank you very much." Helen was shocked to hear Cathy this way; she was usually the strong one in situations like these. It was as though she was completely broken. "Look, I'm coming over with the car straight away, you come and stay with us for a bit, there's no use being on your own, is there?"

Cathy shook her head, but didn't speak; she just put the phone down, sat at the bottom of the stairs and waited for Helen to arrive.

Back at the station, Paul Collison was putting his jacket on, getting ready for his chat with Mrs Froggat. Steve came in and slumped into the chair at his desk, he was looking at the incident board, he noticed the three new photographs, Colin's smiling face, and underneath it a picture of his slit throat, next to that Zach's picture, again smiling, and under that, a picture with the four holes in his chest, and lastly a picture of Stuart, with a large axe hole in his chest, but his other photo was not one of him smiling, just frowning, the same way Steve was at this time.

"Where you headed?" Steve realized Paul was dressed ready for outside.

"Come with me if you want to, I'm going to speak to Mrs Froggat, she says that Jarvis character, hasn't come by to do her electrics, looks like he might be missing too." Paul tilted his head to one side, as an invite for Steve to accompany him. "We'll go and find out, shall we? No use moping around here, let's make ourselves useful, hey?" Suggested Paul. They both got up to leave the station, and headed over to Mrs Froggat's place.

Back at the mortuary Shabby had his hands full, with the three fresh bodies that had just been wheeled in to him. They were still clothed in their work uniforms; there was blood from them and from the chickens, they had butchered. The first thing for Shabby was to separate these blood types, he took some from the wound of Colin's neck, and some from his apron, and he placed these on two microscope slides. Shabby placed these to one side for a moment, and proceeded to take samples from Zach and Stuart. Their clothes were then removed, allowing him to perform the autopsies. The bodies were lined up ready for Shabby; his assistant returned to help, she dressed in her gown and mask. As she approached, she placed the receipt on Shabby's desk, she had collected from the Guns and Ammo store.

"The weapons were bought by a Mrs Michaela Deichmann, here's her receipt," she said.

"That's my sister's name, Sara are you sure it's her?" Shabby picked the receipt up and peered at it.

"That is what the shop assistant says, she wasn't mistaken, because she reported that the same lady came back two days later, to buy a hunting knife."

"No, you don't understand, this woman is my sister; she's a Psychiatrist, with a private practice in the City. She wouldn't be the slightest bit interested in weapons like these."

"Well the assistant was adamant; she even gave us this C.C.T.V still as proof."

Shabby snatched the photo from Sara; he shook his head in disbelief.

"I must go and speak to her immediately, these bodies will have to wait!" Shabby stated.

"Very well then Jack," Sara agreed, and after getting undressed from her gown again, began to examine the blood samples on the microscope, while Shabby got himself ready for his journey to his sister's place.

Back in Mortal Dean, Steve and Paul arrived outside the block of flats that Mrs Froggat lived in. They went inside and caught the elevator to the top floor; Mrs Froggat lived at Number 1024. Steve rang the bell and waited, Mrs Froggat shuffled into view from behind the door.

"Who is it?"

"It's Sergeant Collison and Detective Steve Speed, Mortal Dean Police Madam."

She unchained the door and opened it nervously. Both policemen had their warrant cards out ready, she scoured them first before letting them come in.

"I'll make some tea officers," she said as they sat down in the lounge.

"We understand that Mr Luke Jarvis was supposed to call earlier today, but didn't show, is that correct?" Paul asked.

"Yes, that's right my lights are out of action until he comes to fix them, but he hasn't turned up, I tried phoning and paid him already, and with all these murders on the news, thought I ought to report it, not that he's the type to be doing a thing like that, very nice young man he is."

"Has he ever been late for a job before?" Steve asked.

"No Officer, my neighbour was supposed to have some work done too, she hasn't seen him either, he is always reliable you know." Paul made notes, then stood up

"Thanks, Mrs Froggat, and for the tea, we'll head back and do some checking for you," said Paul politely.

They left her and saw themselves out, the two men were looking at each other, and their thoughts were similar.

"He's been missing since at least yesterday afternoon, maybe even before we went around there, let's go back there now and check again?" suggested Steve.

On their way over to Luke's, they drove past the pub, Steve noticed Sean and Phil on the side of the road; they were walking along, singing songs and staggering together.

"At least they're okay, for now," noted Paul.

"I feel that it won't be long, though, before they're next," said Steve.

The pair of them nodded at each other, they refocused on their task of finding Luke. After several minutes driving, they reached Luke's house, pulled the car over and got out.

"Last time we were here, there was freshly laid concrete," said Paul.

"Yeah and Jeremy was smashed into by a cement lorry," reminded Steve.

"Two and two?"

"Makes five!"

Paul immediately pulled out his mobile phone and called the station; Steve walked up the driveway and went to the back garden. He stared at the new concrete when he got there. "Do you really think he may be under there?" Steve asked.

"Nobody's seen hide nor hair of him, at least for a couple of days, if he went on holiday, I'd imagine he would cancel his appointments, bad business not to and Jeremy gave him as an alibi, so he must have thought he was here too," reasoned Paul.

Steve stepped on to the newly laid floor, and stamped down on it.

"Won't be able to dig this up with our bare hands," Steve remarked.

"I've called the team in the City, they're bringing over a resonator, and ultrasound machines, and some equipment used by the Fire Service, when they look for trapped bodies in buildings," Paul assured Steve. "They'll bring some digging machines with them, but we will check first, if somebody is buried down there," he added.

"How long will that take?"

"Hopefully, they'll be here within the hour, so just relax?" The two men continued to check the property for any evidence.

Back in the City, Shabby had arrived at his sister's house. Jack and Michaela didn't see much of each other, following the death of their parents who had died in an earthquake whilst holidaying in Turkey. With Michaela being the eldest child, all inheritance had been bequeathed to her; Jack hadn't even cared about that, as he'd loved his parents unconditionally. They supported him when he wanted to go into Forensic Science; they funded his education, which he was thankful for. Shabby approached the front door of his sister's house, he pulled the chain hanging down in the porch, and it rang like a gong. Several moments later, Michaela came to answer the door; they had similar looking faces, Shabby was the taller of the two, and she was forty-eight, four years older than him. When Michaela opened the door, she was surprised to see her brother.

"Jack, it's been five years, why are you here?"

"A couple of things have been brought to my attention Mickey."

"Then come on in, and go through to the study, we won't be disturbed in there."

Shabby could hear her children running riot in the back parlour, she had three of them, two girls, Sharon aged six and Chevron who has just turned five, she also had an adult son, Craig aged nineteen, who has left the home.

"That would be wise, but I would like to meet my nieces before I go back, is that okay?"

Michaela nodded; and led him into the study; she went to make some drinks. The children frolicked loudly further through the whole house, Michaela allowed the girls to express themselves, as they saw fit, reasoned that they would find their own path to adulthood, without her interfering nonsense. She was stricter however with Craig; he had a sensible head on his shoulders, much like his Grandfather, in reflection. He followed his influence, so much more than anyone's. Michaela came back to the study with Shabby's whiskey over ice, and she'd made herself vodka and tonic, she handed the whiskey to Shabby.

"So please, tell me why you are here, Jack?"

"As you've probably heard on the news, there's been a number of murders in Mortal Dean, seven to be exact, I get the job of studying these victims myself, we also found some weapons from one case in particular, a shot gun and a cross bow, subsequently it has been revealed to me that you bought these weapons," said Shabby bluntly.

Michaela nodded at his revelation, she sat down at the drawing table, and Shabby stood by the window, waiting for her response.

"Aye, I bought some for Emmerich, he wanted them; he's gone on a hunting holiday with his friends for a fortnight."

"So how did they end up at my laboratory, being linked with the death of a decorated soldier?"

She shrugged her shoulders, and blinked unemotionally at Shabby.

"Maybe they were stolen from his car, I don't know, he hasn't called in days, we don't live in each other's pockets, you know that very well yourself Jack."

It was true they did have a certain freedom within their relationship, her husband had an affair once, and she just allowed it to take place, knowing eventually he'd return to her. Michaela did what she pleased, and so did Emmerich, she rose from the high chair she was sitting in and reached for her cigarette case, she offered one to Shabby, who dismissed the gesture, he needed nothing from her. Michaela lit her cigarette regardless; she walked over to her brother, and rested her arm on his shoulder.

"You should see Emmerich, maybe he can shed some light on this for you, if he phones I'll tell him you want to speak to him, unfortunately I've no idea where he's gone or even who his friends are," she coaxed, as though they were children again.

She always managed to smooth Jack's hackles down, whenever he was vexed. That is a mark of a good Psychiatrist, being able to appease people, and make them feel at ease with their selves. Shabby knew she was genuine, and downed the rest of his whiskey; he pushed the empty glass on to the table.

"Look I'll check with Emmerich, and if he can't substantiate your version of events, I'll be coming back here."

She made a praying China-man gesture at him, as if to say be my guest. Shabby went to leave and as he stepped out of the study, his nieces were standing there.

"This is your Uncle Jack; you've heard me talk about him." Introduced Michaela, he cuddled them both where they stood, kissed their foreheads and left without a word. He didn't even turn to acknowledge Michaela, he moved to his car and drove away, still no nearer to solving this case.

Back at Luke's house the equipment had arrived, ready to discover if Luke was under the concrete. The machinery was set up under a tent to protect it all from the wind, which had picked up. There are four rods, set out in a square, placed in the ground surrounding the foundation. Steve and Paul watched with interest, as the experts went about the process, without consulting them. The Fire Service had arrived with the ultrasound machine, they brought this round to the back of the house, the first person to speak was Karen Blind, and she was the technical analyst, brought in to head up the operation.

"We're ready for the experiment now, guys," she said.

"Stand by Karen," her assistant said, and pressed the return button on the computer keyboard. The resonator made one thundering thump, and straight away on the computer screen, the outline of a person's head and shoulders appeared.

"Right get him out of there, shit!" Steve shouted in frustration.

The whole crew scrambled digging equipment to the garden, and began to break the concrete around the buried Luke. This flurry of activity went on for about fifteen minutes, and eventually they pulled Luke's body from the hole, and laid him down on the grass behind.

"Call the Coroner now" ordered Paul, who as senior officer, pulled rank over the situation. Steve walked away from the scene, his head was in his hands, as he was about to sit down on his car bonnet, his phone rang, and it was Shabby. Steve answered it warily, on seeing his name flash up on the phone display.

"Perfect timing," he muttered to himself. "Shabby, we've found Mr Jarvis, buried in his back yard; he's been there for a day or two by the looks of things."

"Okay Steve, I'll return to the labs right now, so meet you there? I need to discuss a few things, that will be a wee bit difficult over the telephone," explained Shabby, and the telephone call ended.

"That makes eight people killed now, one more and the Regional Serious Crime Squad will pile down here and take over," said Steve, as Paul approached him and handed him the crumpled photograph recovered beside the body

"Right that's all four friends then, this killer really didn't hang about, hey?"

He was staring at the photo, his mind wandered back to the time, when he had searched Jez's flat, and he remembered a dust mark where a photo was missing.

"I'll keep this for now, Paul."

He put the photo in his jacket pocket, just then the Coroner's wagon arrived for Luke's body. Their task done, Steve and Paul decided, they would meet Shabby at the labs. They followed the Coroner's wagon to the mortuary, with Luke's body inside. Shabby was fidgeting with some surgical instruments. His assistant Sara appeared in the lab, she walked to him and handed the mobile phone that traffic had sent over, it was in a clear bag.

"Thank you, Sara, can you prep that bay for a new victim please? They've found another one," Shabby asked.

He pointed at an empty space, Sara went over without a word, began with his instructions. There was a noisy bump at the large swing doors to the lab, and Luke's body appeared on its stretcher, Shabby indicated to the porter, where he wanted it put, behind the stretcher were Paul and Steve.

"Traffic phoned and told me they have located the cement lorry, it returned dented and was logged out by a Mr Saul Reading. Graeme had some of your men check out the name; apparently, he moonlights there, but he's a lab technician really at the University. You should check that out?" Shabby explained; he held up the mobile phone, and they both went over to him. Steve took it from Shabby, opened the bag and lifted out the phone; he switched it on and found the last caller list. Top of the list was Luke's name and number, just below that was Rita's.

"That is who Jez was going to see, before he was killed, probably to tip him off about that alibi" said Steve, showing both men the name at the top.

"And here he is laying there, we should have driven quicker," replied Paul.

Steve put the phone back in the bag and handed it back to Shabby, who took it to his desk.

"This man, covered in concrete, and Mr Stanley being killed by a cement lorry, are tied together in the same instance," Shabby offered.

Steve showed Shabby the photograph, that Paul had given him. He held it up and noticed it was of four men, they were all huddled together kneeling in a line, like it was cut from a larger photo of a football team or something, behind were torsos of others, but no faces could be seen. He saw that Richard's face was crossed out.

"It looks like these people were a gang some time ago, I wondered why the killer has worked quickly and killed in a cluster," explained Shabby.

Steve's eyebrows rose with suspicion, at Shabby's comments, he pointed at Richard.

"Why is he the only one crossed out?"

"Maybe it was to show this Luke, he meant business, he had already taken him out of the equation," Shabby answered.

Steve seemed happy with that answer and walked over to Luke, he was disappointed in himself for missing him in his earlier inquiries. A swell of guilt filled him, he turned to his colleagues.

"Do we have anything else we can get our teeth into, any leads we can use with this case?" He asked.

"There is something significant that I should tell you, so listen carefully," said Shabby.

"Tell us then Jack, what are they?"

"The weapons, used in the Joiner case, they were bought, by a woman, Mrs Michaela Deichmann, two days later she bought a hunting knife, exactly like the one used in the Rusdale murder," he explained.

"Have you spoken to this woman then?" Paul asked.

"Yes, she is my sister, Paul, I questioned her about it earlier; she admits buying them for her husband Emmerich, who has conveniently gone on a hunting holiday with friends, but she denies any knowledge about the use of these weapons."

"We need to find this Emmerich, and quickly," said Steve urgently.

They all agreed, and prepared to find Professor Emmerich Deichmann.

Chapter 9

A Father's Right.

(flashback)

When Gerard was born, his mother, Geraldine, was proud that she had produced a son. George Swales however, wasn't convinced he was the father. Before Gerard came along, his Wife had spent two and a half years away from the farm nursing her sick mother. Only when she had fully recovered, Geraldine returned home for good. George had been left to tend to things back at the farm on his own; she'd come back when she could to check on him. The time she spent away from the farm aroused George's suspicions that she was seeing another man. When Geraldine did finally return home, she was so loving towards George, they'd made love quite frequently, so when Gerard came along some nine months later, it was hard for George to prove to himself that Gerard was his, it all felt too convenient though, she came home, and they immediately had a baby. He felt maybe she was covering something up.

The violence towards Gerard didn't start until after his siblings, Gregg and Georgina, arrived, Gregg first and then Georgina sixteen months later. Gerard's mother always doted on him, however George treated Gregg as his true son, he could see his own features in Gregg but none in Gerard, this made him resentful, even Georgina carried his eyes and hair colour, Gerard just looked different, he looked like his mother but not one characteristic was the same as George's. When Gerard turned five, this was when the violence started, he had a nightmare one night, which woke the whole house, his mother rushed to his bedroom, to try and calm him, his brother shared the same room, the screams from Gerard made Gregg hide under his bed covers, and he peeped out cautiously. The nightmare had made Gerard wet his bed with fright. It was the early hours of the morning, two hours before rising for farm duties, George was not happy about it, he came into the bedroom, Geraldine was stripping back the bedclothes, and had removed the boy's pyjamas, George had noticed the strong smell of urine, and George was furious.

"Five years old and you still piss the bed, get and clean yourself up now!"

The flat of his hand slapped at his back as Gerard left the bedroom, this stung him, and a large red whelp of a handprint showed where Gerard had been hit. His mother scurried behind, horrified at her husband's reaction.

"He's had a nightmare, and scared enough already without you towering over him." She scolded, laying into George, as a protective mother should. George gripped her by the throat, and squeezed, she could hardly breathe, and there was fury in his eyes.

"He's your kid, you teach him to respect others while they're sleeping, and retrain him not to piss his bed!"

He threw her to the floor, she crawled away from him and into the bathroom with Gerard and locked herself inside, she was shocked at being assaulted by her husband, he'd never laid a finger on her before then.

"If he does this again, I'll bring my belt to his backside." George shouted through the door.

Everything calmed down for a while, the nightmares waned and his bed-wetting improved. Gerard explained his nightmares to his mother; he'd dreamt that a stalking beast had killed his whole family including her, and he has the same dream every time, but it just gets worse and longer each time he has one, with vivid detail. For a couple of years, she would lay Gerard down to sleep on his side, everyone had a good night's sleep, and his father's rages subsided for a while, he would get the odd smack for being weak or clumsy, but punishment was never meted out to Gregg or Georgina. One night following his ninth birthday, the same nightmare came into his sub consciousness. Gerard thrashed about kicking and screaming loudly, waking his brother first, his mother ran down the landing to his room, she tried waking Gerard to calm him, by this time his father could hear, he grabbed for his belt on the chair, then headed for the commotion at the end of the landing. He entered the room and again the smell of urine hit him, Geraldine had already stripped him down, she knelt between Gerard and George, she knew what would follow, George snapped his belt together making a cracking sound, this sounded loud in the room, Gregg flinched and slunk under his bed covers.

"Out of the way woman, he must be punished, you're too weak boy!"

He grabbed a large lock of Geraldine's hair and he lifted her up with it, he spun her round and threw her out of the door, closing it behind her.

"Don't do this?" She screeched and hammered on the door.

George widened the belt with both hands and picked Gerard up, he was a strong man, so Gerard couldn't struggle, he was turned round and without any hesitation struck Gerard across his back with the belt, the leather slapped around his waist, and the buckle grazed his side, causing a small cut, but leaving a red horse shoe shape on his skin. George swung the belt a second time, the buckle cut and reddened on the other side of Gerard's body.

"Two whips for pissing the bed this time, every time you do it, I add one more whip to the original two."

He left the room; and his wife went in to aid Gerard's sores, it seemed that each time her husband punished her son for being bad, she would get beaten too. Gerard had the nightmare three more times after that, meaning he was whipped a total of twelve times in all.

Then disaster struck the family business, with a salmonella outbreak and people thinking eggs were bad for you. This sent the nation into believing they'd be poisoned by chickens, and it killed George's livelihood, no financial resources were coming in. He was being ruined and turned to alcohol in despair. This fueled even more resentment towards Gerard. George's treatment of Gerard got so bad over time that he was unable to grow into a normal teenager, when he had his final nightmare at thirteen, Geraldine didn't go to him, George had taken a portable cattle prod to Gerard's room, he pressed it to Gerard and tweaked the switch, it carried a current of 12volts, and it gives a small jolt to the nervous system. Because Gerard was soaked from the bed-wetting, it made the shock seem much greater; he shook vigorously for a few seconds while George held the prod to his stomach.

"Perhaps this will stop the pissing, nothing else seems to work," George said, drunk and angry.

With his father attacking him at home, and the kids at school picking on him, this passage of life was a very miserable time for Gerard. That is why he was so awkward in his ways, constantly nervous; he loved his mother and his strong and confident brother, but detested his father and sister. Gerard was shy and retiring but very clever and cunning, he would write good stories and create models of things, his mind was faster than Gregg's but they held a strong bond, his sister however, was distrusting and behaved oddly towards Gerard, much more like her father. At school Gregg and Georgina fitted into their classes without any problems, originally when Gerard came home with his uniform ripped, his father knew he'd been fighting, but instead of marching to the school demanding answers, he gave Gerard a lesson of his own, he got the belt and whipped Gerard with it, on the body, never the face, this meant that the teachers would not see his bruises, so wouldn't contact social services.

George would say: "You're weak Gerard, you should fight back - I would."

And his mother knew that if she had interfered, then she would get punished too.

Towards Gerard's final school year, he'd managed a successful education, studied hard, and kept his sanity in check by getting good grades from his exams. Seven GCSE's in all, six grade A's and one B. He hated sports, as Physical Education was the only class that Colin, Richard, Jez and Luke were together and took with him.

When Gerard was attacked, for the final time, with tar and feathers, Geraldine thought she had to protect her son, so after she had cleaned him up, they pretended to his father that everything was normal. But this incident had tipped Gerard over the edge, so after that final day, he packed a small case of clothes, stole £20 from George's wallet and caught a bus to the City and disappeared. His family searched in vain for him, but when they had found his school clothes left beside the bank of the estuary, they thought he might have drowned and been swept away, so after a few months the police and his family gave up looking, reasoning that he was probably dead by now.

He had arrived in the city, heart pounding, a new adventure waiting, he had been a bit naïve though, the £20 was very quickly spent, meaning he had to sleep rough for the first few weeks, lying in doorways and visiting soup kitchens wherever possible and was starting to despair about things because he hadn't received any guidance in City life and felt very lost.

One afternoon he was sitting begging for money, and a woman came towards him, he looked up, she looked about twenty-eight, and she had a kind face. She was tall and her figure enticed him.

"You don't need to be doing this, you seem reasonably educated, I think you should come with me, do you fancy a cup of tea?" She asked, holding out her hand, Gerard took it and she led him to the nearest café.

"Order what you like, I'll pay for it, come on don't be shy?" Gerard went along the line choosing food and drink; the woman was waiting at the cash register, he showed what he'd selected and the cashier priced it all for him. She said kindly. "Go and sit over there, I'll be over shortly."

He sat down and began to eat, the woman came over to the table, and she just had one coffee.

"You're not a City type are you, where are you from?" She quizzed, as she sat down, Gerard didn't say anything, he shrugged and she looked at him waiting for an answer.

"Not going to tell me, are you?" She drank some of her coffee noticing that he seemed extremely shy.

"Listen, my name is Michaela, I'm a Psychiatrist, you can speak to me, I won't tell a soul and it's all okay," she explained. Gerard smiled at her comforting voice and began to relax.

"I'm Gerard, sixteen years old and I have left home."

She was looking at the boy and noticed some how he resembled her husband in a strange way.

"Listen I can help you with your shyness, if you will let me, you look as though you've been through a lot, at such a young age," she probed. "You should come back to my home, meet my husband, I think he'll like you."

Gerard didn't reply, he finished his food and drank his orange, he tidied up his mess and collected Michaela's cup.

"You don't have to do that, there are people who come and collect them after we're gone," she pointed out. He put the tray back down; she stood up and put her coat on. "Come on, I'll call a taxi and take you home, you shouldn't be on the street, not at your age."

Gerard followed her out onto the street, the taxi she hailed stopped at the pavement; they both got in and drove to her house. On the way, he was looking at this woman opposite him; she was very attractive, kind and generous. She caught him staring at her cleavage, which was revealed by a v necked pullover, she smiled and pulled her coat around herself, he looked away shyly, feeling awkward.

Michaela and Emmerich had met when she was at university, she was a bright young student and he was finishing his doctorate of Psychology, they dated for a year and married after that. He got a job at the University, as a Professor of Psychology, and Michaela used her qualifications to set up as a Psychiatrist, working from home on individual cases, she had five of these at present and Gerard would be her sixth.

The taxi stopped outside her house, she stepped out and held the door open for Gerard, he slowly got out; the driver was paid and chugged off again. The front door of her house was opened by a man in his forties, with broad shoulders, hair starting to grey a little, looking very wise and competent,

"This is my husband Emmerich, Professor Emmerich Deichmann, to give him his full title," said Michaela, introducing him.

"It seems that you are to be my wife's new project, young man," said Emmerich, shaking Gerard's hand.

Michaela frowned at him for the remark he made. Gerard noticed that Emmerich spoke with a hint of German in his accent, however he instantly felt at ease in his presence.

"My husband was from Germany originally, he emigrated to Britain, after his University degree." Dispelling Gerard's inquisitiveness.

They all went to the sitting room, Gerard entered first and sat in a leather chair by the window, Michaela lit her cigarette and sat on the large futon on the right-hand side of the room, Emmerich rang the bell on the wall, by pressing a switch, a few minutes later a man appeared.

"Ah! Franks, make us some tea please, and some hot chocolate for our guest?"

The man went away again after bowing his head to Emmerich, who put on a quilted smoking jacket and sat on the large Queen Anne chair by the fire, it was warm and welcoming. A few moments later and Franks arrived with the drinks, he handed them round and promptly left without a thank you.

"Franks is our butler, he does all the domestic things around here, right now he'll be making you a room upstairs, so when you go up it will be nice and comfortable," said Michaela.

"Don't be shy around here, we like people to express themselves, if you can't we will help you to," said Emmerich.

"Thank you for taking me in, you've been so kind to me," said Gerard in a swell of gratitude.

"Don't worry, you can leave when you like, we just want you to feel better about yourself, if you can open up to us a bit more, that would be a start?" Suggested Michaela.

"I will leave you to it then dear, I must go to prepare my lecture for a class tomorrow," said Emmerich, he kissed Michaela, but she gave no reaction to it.

"It's getting late, why don't you finish that chocolate and I'll take you to your room upstairs?" She suggested. Gerard did what was asked and followed her out of the sitting room and upstairs; she led him to the end room and opened the door.

"Try and rest, tomorrow we begin with what is troubling you, there are five others here just like you, you each have one to one's with me every week, being that you are the last in, you will be treated on a Saturday, all day long, and the rest of the time you may do as you wish," she explained.

Michaela closed the door to and Gerard prepared himself for bed. He got up in the middle of the night to relieve himself, he crept down the hall and noticed the door on the left was open a little, he glanced through the gap, and Michaela was sitting at her dresser, she'd had a hot bath and a towel was wrapped around her, she noticed in the reflection of her mirror, Gerard was peeping through, she unfastened the towel and opened it, exposing her firm breasts to him, she held it open for five seconds and then closed it again, feeling shocked and excited Gerard quickly moved away on seeing her like that and hurried to the toilet, Michaela smiled and then said to herself,

"That should satisfy his curiosity, now he knows what they look like." The following morning, things were a little awkward between them.

Over the next few years she counseled him on their set basis, once a week on a Saturday. His sessions were intense to start with, Michaela had to have him sedated one or two times, whilst under hypnosis, she regressed him back to his early childhood, she discovered his dream, and it had manifested into a kind of stark reality. The dream was a sort of precognition into what was to come, and it did come in the form of Richard, Jez, Luke and Colin, plus the Jones twins, and his father. The problem with his father was the hardest part to solve, the attacks began when he was such a young boy, so these emotions were deeply ingrained, she had to be careful not to get too carried away, she placed layered suggestive therapy into his sub consciousness, enabling him to become confident with talking about the past, blocking them out and forgetting them, this was ongoing for six years, but Emmerich had discovered something while Gerard was staying there. Emmerich had an affair, eighteen months into his marriage; he met a flame haired woman named Geraldine whilst she was nursing her sick mother. He was helping with her burden to start with, giving her a shoulder to cry on. Things grew more personal after that as they will. The affair had lasted for nearly two years, then her mother got better and she had to return to her husband and he returned to Michaela. What he didn't realize then was; Geraldine had become pregnant with his baby and had to hurry back home to cover it up. Emmerich didn't even know she was married, he always assumed she was single. Gerard's mannerisms were similar and he had Geraldine's hair and eye colour. He performed a test on himself and secretly took some of Gerard's DNA, when the results returned to him positive; he was astonished to learn that he was Gerard's biological father.

He asked Michaela to let him sit in on one of her counselling sessions and listened in horrified detail to what Gerard was telling her, about the beatings by George, the dreams he'd been having, the burning from the Jones twins, the horrible things the four boys were doing to him. After that session, he said to Gerard.

"Seeing as this was your only session with me, I must conclude that having suffered at the hands of your peers for so long and at such prolonged sequences. I am astonished at your demeanour, if it had been me, I would not have coped so well, I would have thought of ways to seek revenge on these people. My admiration goes out to you, but somehow you must seek closure on this chapter of your life. If you don't, then you will never fully recover from these episodes of violence towards you. Good luck to you, I hope in the future I can be of further assistance to you."

Emmerich decided he would drive to Mortal Dean, and went straight to the High School. He asked the Head Teacher, for details of the children from Gerard's year. There wasn't any mention of bullying, and no reports of abuse from home regarding Gerard. Emmerich was appalled by this, and asked for photographs, the Head obliged of course.

While he was there in Mortal Dean, he visited Mrs Sheila Jones; he pretended to be a modelling agent and was looking for a set of twins, to model some clothes for him. Mrs Jones gave him one photo of Betty and Caitlin; he also visited Brown Gale and drove down the farm lane to see the Swales family. When Geraldine recognized Emmerich, she couldn't hide her joy, he put his hand over her mouth to silence her, she took him to the kitchen, and they kissed passionately for a while, it had been twenty-two years since last seeing one another. He broke off the kiss to ask her for a photograph of her husband George, she didn't even question why and handed the one on the kitchen cabinet to him.

"The next time I come, I'll take you away from here," he promised.

"Who is this then mum?" Asked Gregg when he saw them.

"This is Professor Deichmann, he is interested in how we operate on a farm," she explained. Gregg walked back out and began his work on the farm, allowing Emmerich to sneak another kiss from Geraldine, and she responded.

Following his return from Mortal Dean he devised a plan to aid Gerard. In his plot for vengeance, his anger had consumed him completely and he shut himself away in his study, for days he was in there not answering to anyone, he couldn't believe the treatment of his son, they all treated him like a dog and they were going to be punished.

The following Saturday, he waited for Michaela's session to begin with Gerard, he listened as she put him under hypnosis, relaxing him and coaxing him into a trance, Emmerich instructed Franks the butler, to tell Michaela that she has a telephone call when he gives the signal; once the trance was successful, Franks entered her study, she looked round at him.

"Sorry Madam, you have an urgent telephone call, from the hospital," he said.

"Very well then," she replied and followed him out to take the call.

While she was away, Emmerich crept in and went over to Gerard; he stroked his forehead and said: "Gerard, while you are at peace with yourself, you will not think too strongly of the people who treated you badly, but if I were to show you photographs of these people, then this will make you so angry, that you'll want to harm them, treat them in the same manner as they have treated you." Emmerich continued with his subliminal message, he came around to face Gerard, who was lying flat on his back, gazing straight up at the ceiling. "When I count from ten you will fall into a deeper sleep," which is what Emmerich did. "And now I'm going to count up to ten, you will not remember this conversation," he began to count up. "You will respond normally to Dr Deichmann's treatment, eight, nine, ten, and relax," said Emmerich, before creeping out and returning to his own study; where he began cutting the photos of people he'd collected. When Michaela returned, she wasn't aware of anything wrong in the room, she continued with the session as usual.

Later Emmerich told Gerard about the DNA test, revealing that he was his real father, Gerard accepted this graciously but Michaela didn't, she knew there was an affair, but couldn't believe it was with Gerard's own Mother, such coincidences, or was it fate? She agreed to finish Gerard's treatment and after another four years, she thought it was successful. Everything seemed to die down for a bit, Gerard worked in a lot of different jobs, gaining vital experience, his confidence was high, he had found and been accepted by his real father and was happy.

Ten years later, Emmerich was ready to begin with his plan; the first session was with the photograph of the Jones twins; he counted down from ten and put Gerard into his trance. He then positioned Gerard so that he sat facing a slide projector screen, and slid the photo of Betty and Caitlin under the light, Gerard focused on the picture; these girls were smiling at him.

"See how they laugh son? They burn you and then laugh at you, how could you let them get away with this?" Emmerich could see the anger rise, right up through Gerard and hit the surface. "Something has to be done, you must take them out," he suggested, then gave detailed instructions of what to do, where the twins would be, etc., then handed his son the bag containing the petrol, fireworks and rope along with his car keys.

Later that night when Gerard returned, Emmerich de-briefed him then brought him out by counting back up from one to ten.

Emmerich even asked his own wife to buy the weapons he needed for Richard's execution and told her he was going on a hunting holiday in a secluded cabin, with friends, which gave him time and privacy to prepare Gerard for his next attacks.

The same method was used for Richard, Luke and Jeremy, well he was a lucky accident, Emmerich hadn't planned on him being on the road where Gerard could take him out whilst escaping in the cement lorry – and Colin; Emmerich felt no remorse about Zach and Stuart, they were just two pawns who had got in the way of his master plan. Each time, Gerard was put under hypnosis, the pictures shown, instructions and any equipment given, and off Gerard went on Emmerich's twisted mission of vengeance for his son and when he returned, Emmerich enjoyed the gory details before bringing him round; and he'd kept his hands clean throughout it all.

Saturday night, they had a few drinks; Gerard felt relaxed sitting in the cabin that they had booked for this holiday. Suddenly Emmerich began counting down from ten again, Gerard began to feel sleepy, Emmerich got to five, Gerard could hardly keep his eyes open, the counting got to zero and Gerard was completely under Emmerich's command again. Emmerich slid the photo of George Swales under the light, and Gerard was turned to face it on the wall.

"See this man, pretending to be your dad, remember how he treated you, how he humiliated and tortured you? He doesn't have the right to do that, he isn't your father - I am. I'm asking you to go to the farm, find him, teach him a lesson in humility," suggested Emmerich. The fury in Gerard's body was beginning to boil over; he rose from his chair, dressed in his long black shiny coat, pulled up the hood after wrapping the scarf around his face; he was ready. Emmerich gave the keys to Gerard, who snatched them from him and sped off in the Land Rover to tackle George Swales.

Over in Mortal Dean, the Swales were starting their dispatch of fresh live chickens, Gregg as usual did the driving, and he was waiting for the load to be finished. Georgina was carrying the hens in crates, they were flapping and squawking inside when the last of the load was put on and the wagon secured. Gregg began to drive off; Gerard sat in the Land Rover waiting for the wagon to disappear from view, he watched Georgina go into the hen yard, as she went out of sight, Gerard got out of his vehicle and went over to the largest barn on the farm, he found his old metal bedstead, and stood it up against the wall, under a 3-phase power source, he disconnected the power and wired two copper cables to the power supply, he looked about the barn for the metal shackles, when he'd found them, he placed them on the workbench by a door, together with an old pitchfork with the wooden handle broken off; he now had the materials he needed and preceded to find George. It was late at night so he'd probably be asleep, bypassing his mother cooking in the kitchen, Gerard went upstairs and walked to George's room, there he was fast asleep, snoring and smelling of Irish whiskey, Gerard crept to the wardrobe and opened it, inside were a selection of ties and belts, he instantly found the belt that George used to beat him with, the thick black leather one with the brass horseshoe buckle, he put this between his teeth. Then he pulled the old man up still sleeping and lifted him onto his shoulders and carried him back downstairs. His mother hadn't heard a thing and continued with her sandwich making. Gerard felt so strong and powerful, his rage surging through him. He stood George up against the bedstead, put the shackles around his ankles and wrists, then wound copper wire around his torso, around his neck he tied the belt through the bedstead. He left George for a moment, and began tying more wire to the metal half of the pitch fork, he then lifted this up and rested some old guttering slanted downwards at George, so when Gerard let go of the wire, it would slide down and jam into the bedstead, making an electrical circuit. The final task was to fetch a bucket of water, this was done and his trap was ready. Gerard then roused George by waving some smelling salts under his nose, he sniffed awake and was startled by the figure standing before him.

"Who are you, what's happening?"

Gerard picked up the bucket of water and threw it at George, soaking him completely, he spluttered as the water ran down his face. Gerard lowered his hood and unwrapped the scarf, revealing himself and looked down at George, over the past twenty years he had grown tall and strong.

"Hello Dad, it's been a while, I've brought you down to ask you a few things, it's okay, Mum doesn't know we're here," said Gerard. George was surprised to hear him speak, and began to wrestle with his shackles.

"Suppose you tell me what it was that I did that was so bad, that you had to punish me the way you did?"

"You're not my son, I've always known that, the bitch had somebody while she was away, I couldn't raise another man's child, it's not right," George whined. Gerard had found the cattle prod that had been used on him those many years ago, he pressed it to George's belly and flicked the switch, it sizzled on his skin, George gave out a scream, he looked at Gerard, who was seething with rage.

"Tell me why you beat me then, why I was punished by you, and never given a chance?" Gerard reached up for the wire above his head and held on to it; he looked at George, waiting for his explanation.

"I was trying to make a man out of you, you're a weakling, my old man did it to me, I was just passing his discipline on to you; a father has a right to punish his children, without being judged by others."

"You are not my father, you never were and you never will be, Emmerich Deichmann is my father." As he spoke, Gerard pulled the wire he was holding, to switch on the power supply that crackled into use; his other hand was holding the release of the pitchfork.

"Goodbye George, see you in hell!"

Gerard released the pitchfork, it slid down the chute and slammed into George's midriff, it made a connection through his body on to the bedstead, 450 volts of electricity shot through his body, and because George was wet, arced right through him, he shook and contorted with pain, his hair was smoking; his body looked tight and blotchy. Seconds more and the power blew out, leaving George stood there in absolute silence. He wasn't breathing any more, Gerard looked at him for a few moments, then turned to leave.

Geraldine had gone to see where George had got to, he wasn't in his bedroom, so she searched the farm, she had picked up Bill the farm cat and walked out into the yard when she saw sparks coming from the barn and went over. She peeked through the hole in the door and witnessed the whole thing happening. As Gerard turned to leave, he looked straight at her and smiled; he put his fingers to his lips and said, "Sssh!"

Geraldine smiled, she was pleased to see him again and her pride rose through her, she watched him as he sprinted to the Land Rover, where he turned, smiled at her again and drove off, she waited, unsure of her feelings, for forty minutes before going in and calling the police.

Gerard drove away fast, adrenalin was pumping through his body and it didn't take him long to reach his father's cabin, he parked up the Land Rover and went into the cabin. Emmerich stood, guided Gerard back to the table and sat him down.

"Did you complete your mission?"

"Yes, Father."

Emmerich began to count back up to ten.

"One, two, three, four, five." Gerard started to come back around. "Six, seven, eight, nine, ten." Emmerich clicked his fingers and Gerard was wide-awake again, oblivious to what he had just done.

"We've got to leave today my son, and quickly." The two men gathered up their food and clothing; locked the cabin, Emmerich broke a window and packed the car, then drove back to the City to cover their tracks.

Chapter 10

Sergeant's Hunch

Shabby, Paul and Steve arrived at Michaela's house; Shabby decided he would wait in the car while Steve and Paul questioned her. They rang the bell and Steve turned around to look back at the car.

"You don't think he has something to do with this, do you Paul?" He asked.

"I don't think anything right now pal, I'm keeping an open mind," replied Paul.

Just then the door opened and an attractive woman was standing before them.

"I am Doctor Michaela Deichmann, how can I help?" She asked; Paul showed his warrant card, which she read.

"We know who you are, your brother is here with us, he's thinks that we ought to ask you some questions," Steve explained.

"Questions? That sounds serious, I hope that I can answer them for you, do come in," she said coolly. She led the way inside and sat the men in the study, then said.

"I'll order some tea for us," and disappeared for a moment, when she returned, she was smoking a cigarette and carrying a silver tray, which she placed on the ottoman in front of them, she sat slowly in a high chair opposite the two men. Steve surveyed her beauty, studying her figure, he could almost make out her breasts, pressing through the material of her blouse, her legs were crossed and he could see the creamy skin of her thighs. Michaela noticed Steve looking and composed herself in a less sensual way.

"As you are probably aware from the media, there's been eight murders in Mortal Dean, at least two of these murders have been linked to you because you bought weapons similar as the ones used and we would like to get to the bottom of it all," Steve began.

"Oh dear, my brother's never been very good at explaining things, even when we were children," she said, her demeanour was vacant and disinterested, puffed on her cigarette, anticipating the next question.

"Why did you buy these weapons, Dr Deichmann?" Paul asked politely.

"Just as I have explained to Jack, I bought them for my husband, he specifically wanted these for his hunting trip, don't you buy things without condition for your wife, Sergeant?" She queried.

"I'm not married anymore, but, yes I suppose I would, but we are not here to question me," came his reply.

"Listen, I went to Guns and Ammo on his insistence, to buy a crossbow and shotgun, he was going on a hunting holiday to this cottage in the middle of nowhere with some colleagues of his and he gave me very precise specifications, I was only acting as a gopher," she reiterated. "If they have been used to kill somebody, that certainly isn't anything to do with me and I doubt if it's anything to do with him. I have five clients staying here at the house that need my counsel daily, they are highly emotional kids who need their confidence back but, if asked, will verify that I have been here just about permanently for the last three weeks," she said.

"Very well, Dr Deichmann, can Steve have a quick word with them?" Paul pressed.

"Just don't ask about individual's cases, they are of the strictest confidence," Michaela responded, Paul nodded at Steve,

"You go," Michaela opened the door and led the way out; Paul remained in the study, he stood up, walked around and studied the photos dotted about on the walls and desk. Steve and Michaela went up to the next floor of the house; she stopped at the first door and knocked on it.

"There are five very vulnerable children here with us, so go easy on them, some are extremely shy, others have been here longer and are a bit more confident," she explained as the door opened, it was a girl, dressed in a flannel bed robe. Steve noticed that her figure was one of a fully-grown woman and quickly averted his eyes as Michaela introduced her.

"This is Sally Kendrick, she is fourteen, her mother and father were killed by a lorry driver, leaving her orphaned," said Michaela.

"Hello Sally, I'm Steve, can you tell me if Dr Deichmann has been here for the last three weeks, please?"

She nodded her head, turned and closed her door. The next door that Michaela knocked on politely, opened.

"This is Daniel Brown, thirteen, he was abused by two gay men, and used as a prostitute by them," she said.

"Good evening Daniel, can I ask you if the Doctor has been here for the last three weeks?" Inquired Steve.

"Yes, she has, I had my session yesterday and last week, plus the previous Monday." Daniel answered. Steve nodded and Daniel closed the door again, he realized that Michaela was telling the truth.

"Do you want to question all of the children or just get a consensus?" She asked. "You know it is quite late at night, they shouldn't really be disturbed."

Steve slipped his arm around the Doctor and said.

"I don't believe it was you who killed those people, but somebody wants to place you as an accessory to that fact, you need to think about who this could be."

She hadn't moved away from his advance, and she looked in his handsome eyes, Michaela suddenly kissed him fully on the lips, Steve was pleasantly surprised by this and responded by moving his hand to her right breast, slipping his hand into a gap between her blouse buttons; stroked one of the erect nipples that he had been looking at earlier for about two seconds, before regaining his senses and moving away.

"I'm sorry doctor, I am happily married, you took me by surprise for a moment," he said awkwardly.

"She obviously hasn't touched you in years and my husband has neglected me for far too long, I saw you looking at me, you want me, I want you, we both need this," she said seductively moving her hand to his crotch and feeling his hardness beneath his trousers, she squeezed firmly for a second.

"One for you and one for me," She said, smiling. They moved away from each other and went back down to the study and joined Paul.

"The Doctor's telling the truth Paul, the children have vouched for her," said Steve.

"Okay Dr Deichmann, we'll leave it there, thank you," said Paul. She nodded, and led the men back out to the hall passage, Steve looked at her, lust rising within him, she acknowledged his thought with a cool smile.

"Don't worry, we'll find your husband and get to the bottom of this," said Paul as she closed the door on the men, who returned to the car, as they got there, Shabby was on the car phone.

"Come on get in, there's been another one!" He shouted as they scrambled quickly to the car and sped off.

"Who is it this time, Shabs?" Paul asked.

"Old man George Swales, from Brown Gale Farm, found dead in his barn by his Wife," explained Shabby.

Steve looked across at him feeling a bit guilty for thinking he could have killed someone. All of Steve's leads have been dead ends so far, he was feeling a mixture of emotions, guilt about his friend and anger that somebody else was killed while their backs were turned, added to the fact that he'd been felt up by a beautiful woman. The memory of her cool eyes, taut nipple and firm squeeze made Steve swerve the car on the road; making the other two men clutch parts of the interior with anxious looks on their faces.

"Whoa! Steady on Steve, we want to get there in one piece, mate," corrected Paul. He slowed down and applied a bit more concentration to his driving.

When they arrived at Brown Gale, it was after midnight, Shabby got out first, and went over to Geraldine who was standing by the front door of the farmhouse, when she saw Shabby, she approached, still holding Bill the cat,

"Sorry for our late arrival, Mrs Swales, can you tell us as much as you know, please?" Shabby asked, stroking the cat, which jumped out of her arms and ran away.

"The main barn, electric flashes, I went over and it was George, he was against the wall, sparks coming out of him, there was this man watching, he didn't even help him, just watched him die," she answered, barely coherent.

"Can you describe this man?" He questioned again.

"Long black shiny coat with the hood up, white scarf over his face, powerfully built."

"The same character as before," said Steve, who had just come across, Shabby nodded in agreement, the two men walked with Geraldine to the barn, Paul was already there, checking that the power was off.

"Okay, it's safe to come in now," said Paul.

"This man is absolutely fried. Why has he been tied to this bedstead? Why is there a belt around his neck? Why the cattle prod? – Was it torture or to get information? Are these materials significant to the perpetrator in some way? Did the victim know his attacker?" Shabby conveyed his thoughts out loud, again into the Dictaphone.

Meanwhile Paul had found some bolt cutters in the barn and he was busy cutting the shackles from George's feet and wrists, he was wearing gloves so as not to contaminate anything. They had to lay George down on the floor; with the pitchfork still sticking out of him, his skin had been fused to the metal of the bedstead.

"You'll have to cut around his body to free him, I will call the Coroner again," suggested Shabby.

Paul began to cut the metal and Steve was studying the trap, Geraldine was standing beside Shabby, while he made his phone call, as he finished he turned to Geraldine and asked.

"Where are your children Mrs Swales? Were they here when this happened?"

She stood and looked out of the barn door, she pointed up the yard to the chickens' enclosure.

"My daughter Georgina is up there working and my son Gregg is delivering his hens to the factory, he should be back soon," she explained.

"They don't know about this yet then?"

Geraldine shook her head; her face showed no emotion about the death of her husband, Shabby made a mental note.

"We should find your daughter and tell her," suggested Shabby, so they went out to look for Georgina in the chicken sheds.

"Georgie, where are you?"

Just then a picture of absolute heaven walked into view, Shabby felt a little bit shy upon seeing her. Georgina; thirty-two years old, six feet tall, had an hourglass figure, her reddish-brown hair flowed down to the middle of her back, she was wearing a flowing skirt, a lilac silk blouse and on her feet, were blue Wellingtons with pictures of chickens on them. Her hazel eyes pierced right through Shabby as she studied him.

"Who is this, Mum?" She asked, her voice mesmerizing Shabby, he felt like a little boy before her.

"Darling this is Jack Stores, there has been an incident at the main barn, your Dad's been killed," replied her mother; once again Shabby noted the lack of emotion.

"I am part of the Forensic Science team, a Pathologist. I examine crime scenes and I'll be piecing together the evidence for this case," Shabby explained, regaining some composure before this vision, she had some tears in her eyes but she wasn't sobbing about the news of her father.

"So, it's murder then? You do realize that this has been hanging over Dad for years, ever since my brother disappeared," said Georgina.

Geraldine moved to silence her. "She doesn't know what she's saying, she's in shock," defended Geraldine. Shabby knew when people were shocked, and quickly realized that Georgina wasn't.

"Why don't we go to the house, it will be more comfortable, so we can talk more in depth?" He suggested, eager to hear more from this angelic voice as they were walking back down to the house, Gregg arrived in his wagon, parked and got out, when he saw the activity going on in the barn, sprinted over to see what was going on inside. What he saw made him shout out, Steve and Paul had to restrain him, preventing him from being by his father's side.

"You can't go near him Sir, the scene needs to be preserved as it is, we can't allow you to touch him, you will leave fibres all over him," Paul explained and Gregg stopped forcing his way in.

"Listen, I will wait for the Coroner, why don't you go with Mr Swales to the house, try and calm him down, ask him some questions," Steve suggested. Paul agreed and walked off with Gregg to the house, when they reached the kitchen, the other three people were already there sitting at the large table in the centre of the room, Shabby noticed the difference between the brother and sister's emotions, Gregg was a broken man, and Georgina was stoic and unfazed by it all.

"It will be a while before the Coroner can get here, so let's try and gather some information, which may help us with this awful crime," suggested Shabby. Geraldine spoke first.

"I said it before, a man in a long black coat, he electrocuted my husband, then just watched him die and ran off!"

"What was the man driving? Did you see the registration plate?" Shabby asked.

"It was a dark coloured Land Rover, but the plate was muddy, so I didn't see the number," she answered. Shabby saw that the vein in her neck was vibrating, and knew she was lying, but he didn't press her again for answers. His attention then moved to Georgina, he was looking at her sexy hazel eyes.

"You said something up on the farm about your brother, what did you mean by that?" He asked.

"You said he was murdered, my Dad, right? Well if anybody wanted him dead, I would say it would have to be our older brother Gerard, he's been missing for twenty years," she reasoned. Shabby wouldn't be able to tell if she was lying or not, she melted him with each gaze.

"Your brother is dead Georgie, stop saying things like that, please," snapped Geraldine. Shabby noticed the vein was vibrating again, she knew something that her kids did not.

"What about you Gregg, what do you think?" Asked Paul.

"I would say if it was Gerard, then why wait all this time, he did awful things to Gerard, our Dad, but he wouldn't bear a grudge for so long, I know my brother," said Gregg.

"Maybe it was an old friend of his, he did borrow a lot of money once, but never fully paid him back, perhaps it was him," explained Geraldine.

"Can you give us a name then please, Mrs Swales?" Asked Paul.

"Yes, I can, his name is Bernard Sirtes, he owns the chicken factory but he doesn't live in Mortal Dean," she answered, desperately trying to buy some time before they worked out her Gerard was still alive and kicking.

Steve came into the kitchen and motioned to Shabby. "The Coroner is here, he wants to speak to you." All five stood and came with Shabby to meet with the Coroner.

"You three, don't plan any holidays for a while, we may need you for further questioning," ordered Paul.

"We must take the body to the hospital first, to remove this metal from his back, he's been dead for about two to three hours, Jack," said the Coroner.

"Very well, bring him over to the mortuary when that's done," said Shabby. The Coroner nodded and returned to his wagon.

Paul faced the entire Swales family and said. "It may be a while before you can arrange his funeral, you know I will try my best to get his killer brought to book, for what he's done to you."

Gregg shook Shabby by the hand, and then Shabby looked over to Georgina.

"I would like a chance to speak to you again, please Miss Swales? Here's my card, call me if you would like to chat," she looked at him with curious eyes, and then smiled.

"I would certainly like to call you, if I have any information," she replied. Shabby was starting to fall for this beautifully formed woman; Steve had to pull him away from her gaze.

"Come on Casanova, that's enough of that," Steve whispered.

They left the Swales to their grief, or lack of it, and drove back to the police station; Steve dropped Paul off and proceeded to drive Shabby to the Mortuary. The next morning Paul was sitting at his desk and he was looking at the incident board, at least he now knew, that the person they were looking for was a man, and two possible names had entered the frame, he rose from his chair and went over to the board. He wrote Bernard Sirtes and Gerard Swales' name down, under the artists' impression of the killer. He quickly remembered that Steve had a photo in his desk, he went over and opened the drawer, and there it was a photo of Gerard Swales, tied up and looking sad. Paul took this and put it in his pocket, he went to the custody offices and approached Simon. Paul showed Simon the photo, and said.

"Scan this photo into the computer will you, when you've done that, age the picture twenty years would you please, add a bit of weight to it, he looks like a scarecrow?" Simon looked at him, puzzled by the request, but did what he was asked, he placed the photo on the scanning machine and it began to appear on the computer screen, Simon then asked the computer to age it by twenty years, clicked the mouse and hey presto! Gerard Swales appeared on the screen, thirty-six years old.

"Good, print a dozen of those off for me," ordered Paul.

Thirty seconds later the photos fed out of the printer, Paul smiled and took one.

"Thank you, Simon, carry on with your business," said Paul, putting the old photo back in Steve's drawer, keeping a new one all for himself.

He went to the car park and took one of the pool cars for a drive, he was going to question the victims' families again, hopefully showing them the new photo, would jog their memories. His first place was Mr and Mrs Jones; he parked outside their flat and took the elevator up. Paul rang the bell, and Jim Jones answered, he instantly moved back to allow Paul in, Sheila was sitting down on the sofa, when Paul came in she moved over, and he sat down.

"I hope things are okay, I have come again, just to ask you one thing, who do you think this might be?" Paul asked, showing her the photograph.

"My word that looks like that creepy Gerard Swales, doesn't it darling, but isn't he dead?" Jim nodded with agreement, at his wife's observations.

"My daughters didn't get on particularly well with him, Sergeant," explained Jim.

"It may just be, that he's responsible for their murder, Mr Jones," said Paul. "And he might not be dead, if we can confirm sightings of him recently, then we may be on his trail," he added. Sheila and Jim looked at each other with pleased expressions; then Paul spoke out again.

"There was another killing last night, old man George Swales, killed at his home, something that the daughter said, has triggered this line of enquiry you see." He put the photo back in his folder, and made his way out, both Joneses followed him on to the landing, Sheila said.

"I am glad someone is interested in solving this, good luck Sergeant." With a nod, Paul left the flat.

His next visit would take him to Cathy French's house, on the way over he had an air of confidence, about solving these bizarre events. He arrived outside of Cathy's house and as he walked to the front door, he noticed that the lawn hadn't been mowed for nearly three weeks. He had a small tut to himself; his grass was cut every two days at home. He rang the doorbell and Cathy stumbled to the door in her drunken state, she opened the door clumsily, she was still wearing her dressing gown, and smelt of Gin.

"Hello Sergeant, how are you? I'm pleased to see you," she slurred.

"Thank you, Miss French, I'm fine, I want to ask you a question or two, okay to come in?" He asked.

Cathy stepped back and turned on the spot, to allow Paul entry and she continued into the kitchen as Paul followed. Paul put the kettle on for himself, Cathy just sat clutching her glass, while the kettle boiled he took off his coat, brought out the photograph and put it on the table, Cathy leaned over in her drunken haze to look at the photo.

"Yes, I know him, he's Gerard Swales, or Outlaw as Ricky and Jez would call him, when we all went to school together, they picked on him a bit," she explained.

"Right I see, we have reason to believe that he might still be alive and that he may have killed Richard and Jeremy, Cathy," revealed Paul.

"No, I don't believe that, he was a timid boy and wouldn't hurt a fly," said Cathy.

"But it is him in the picture, right? So, it could be a possibility," reasoned Paul.

"If it is Gerard, I'll tear him apart myself, he deserves it after all," hissed Cathy and began to cry again, remembering Richard, Paul held her close for a minute, then broke off and made his goodbyes.

Paul left Cathy's house, returned to his car, and made his way to the Stanleys, when he arrived outside their house, he glanced over at Steve's place and noticed his Mercedes in the driveway. He continued to the front door of the Stanley house, Zane was racing around crazily in the back garden, he rang the bell and Helen answered, she smiled at him. Helen and Paul had been an item for many years, even before she met Jeff.

"I've come here on police business, I need to ask a question," said Paul. She opened the door wide and led him into the lounge, she left to make tea, when she returned to him minutes later; Helen lit a cigarette and then sat down.

"Listen Helen, I have a photo and wouldn't mind knowing who you think it might be, and if you may have seen him before, perhaps hanging around," he offered the photograph; she took it, looked at it and nodded.

"Yes, I know who this is, my daughter has him on her mobile phone, he goes to her gym, this is just like one she took about three weeks back. Apparently, he's very athletic and uses all the apparatus in the gym," she pointed out.

"Very interesting, cause a few people round here say he died twenty years ago," Paul explained.

"No, he is definitely on her phone, look, I'll show you," said Helen, she went and got Jordanna's phone from the side table, she sifted through a few moments and then she said.

"See there he is, plain as day, he calls himself Gerry." Paul nodded as the comparisons were made to his photo; the only differences between the two were that Gerard had dyed his hair black, and grown a stylish jaw-line beard and thin moustache to match. Paul put the picture back in the folder.

"Well this man could be responsible for Jeremy's death, the latest victim is old man Swales, and this man in your daughter's phone is one Gerard Swales, see why I came here," explained Paul. Helen quickly sat down again in shock; Paul didn't console Helen this time and went to leave.

"Sorry Helen, this looks like a break through, I've got to go and see Steve, so if you could excuse me, I'll see myself out," said Paul. "Try and stay positive, it won't be long before we track this guy down, give my regards to Jeff."

He crossed the road and walked up Steve's driveway, rang the doorbell, Brenda answered the door, Paul got the same warm smile as the other three women did before, he sniffed at his aftershave, maybe that was doing it for him.

"Steve, it's Sergeant Collison dear, he's here to see you," she called. Steve came to the front door and ushered Paul out into the Garden.

"I don't like police talk in front of the wife, let's have it here?" Steve asked.

"Look at this, this is the photo in your desk drawer, but I have had it brought up to date by twenty years, and Jordanna Stanley has got a similar one of a "Gerry" on her mobile, he may be responsible for what's going on around here," explained Paul. Steve frowned, he'd forgotten about that photo of Gerard, he snatched the photo and glared at it.

"Let's try to find this creep then, and Dr Deichmann's husband," said Steve. Paul took the photo back off him and put it in his jacket.

"I reckon it is of the utmost urgency that we find these two people, give Shabby a call, he can visit his sister again, maybe she can narrow down where his hunting cottage might be," ordered Paul.

"Shabby has his hands full at the moment, at the morgue, I'll pay Michaela a visit tomorrow myself," said Steve.

"I'll send Simon on to question this Bernard Sirtes, just in case," Paul added.

"I think we should cross him off the list, I feel it was a name thrown in by Mrs Swales, she was very edgy when we were there. I am surprised you didn't notice," said Steve.

"She was acting funny when the daughter was saying stuff about her brother," Paul noted.

"She certainly turned Shabby's head," said Steve.

"We should turn in for the day, and start fresh tomorrow morning, what do you think?" Suggested Paul. Steve was happy with that, slapped Paul on the shoulder, and went back indoors.

Paul took the car back to the station, very pleased with his day's work. Steve sat in his lounge thinking of this breakthrough, he knew that finding Gerard and Emmerich would make things a whole lot easier for him. He would begin with a visit to Michaela's place; she would at least know where he might be found. He decided to turn in for the night, and get an early start.

Chapter 11

Rescue, therapy, and condition.

Jordanna Stanley, former champion gymnast, comfortably off from endorsements, still used the Feel Gorgeous Gym to tone herself twice a week. Phil Barker and Sean Curle also use the same gym, they both fancied themselves as beefcakes and when they weren't at work in the Mortal Dean chicken factory, they were here bulking up and strutting their stuff. Gerry Swales usually attended three times a week, using all the equipment to keep himself in prime condition. This evening, all four of them were in. Jordanna was on a rowing machine; she'd been using this for thirty minutes or so, loving the swinging motion of the exercise. Phil and Sean were using the weight machines as usual, but they stopped their exercises to watch Jordanna moving rhythmically backwards and forwards on her machine, after watching her working for quite a while, Phil nudged Sean and said.

"I want a piece of that, look at that body, let's try and pull her after we're done here, maybe she'll do us both."

Sean was a little more reserved.

"Listen Phil, I don't want to spoil the mood or anything, but that is Jez's sister, I don't fancy doing what you're suggesting, out of respect for him, let's just give it a miss this week," said Sean.

Their usual 'method' was to complete their circuits, pick out a woman they fancied at the gym, follow her to a bar, one would chat her up, get her drunk and bring her to a hotel, whilst the other would be waiting, then she would be persuaded into a threesome. They've done this nearly every week for five years very successfully.

"Don't be stupid, she's right for us, you know the routine, it was your turn last week, now it is my turn this week," Phil added, he'd always had an influence over Sean, a way of getting him to do what he wanted.

Five years ago, Phil had caught his sister having sex in the hallway of his flat with Sean, he'd walked in on them and taken photos of them on his phone, now he uses this as leverage in his plans by threatening to show his father (who has a vicious temper and several convictions for violence), pictures of Sean with his "princess". Sean knew there would be no way out of it as Phil still had the footage on his phone, so he reluctantly agreed to go along with the idea on condition he wouldn't touch Jordanna. They watched her flowing backwards and forwards on the rowing machine, Phil was steadily getting more turned on by it. What Phil and Sean didn't know was that Jordanna liked men watching her, she was aware of her own body image and proud to show how supple she was. Jordanna slowed her exercising to warm herself down.

"Hey, let's go to the shower room and get some pictures of her, we haven't done that for ages, what do you think?" Phil suggested.

Sean made no protest and followed his friend to the shower room, just as they disappeared, Gerard entered the gym, he had a rigorous routine planned, wanting to tone every inch of his body which he hadn't for two and a half weeks, whilst on holiday with his father, he felt stiff, unfit and flabby. He began with a few chin ups, Jordanna had stopped her rowing and grabbed her towel for a deserved shower, she saw Gerard effortlessly pull himself up on the chin bar, he paused for a few seconds, and smiled at her, she smiled back and left for her shower, Gerard moved on to the next apparatus, to do some sit ups, followed by the bench press, beginning with pressing 75kg to start with.

In the shower room Phil and Sean had climbed into the ceiling, leaving enough of a gap between tiles to peer through. Jordanna came into the showers, oblivious to her audience, she wiped off the sweat on her neck and shoulders, then her long legs, Phil started breathing heavily, he got his mobile phone out of his tracksuit pocket, he held it ready to see more of her. Jordanna sat down on the changing bench, she took her t-shirt off, Phil and Sean could see her breasts encased in her sports bra underneath.

"Come on take it off," whispered Phil, he was working himself up about it all, while Sean was starting to worry for Jordanna, with both hands she reached round her back, her chest pushed up as she did this, she released the clasp and took off the bra. Phil took a picture of Jordanna's breasts as they heaved up towards him, but he wanted the whole package, and lay poised to see her take off the shorts, before Jordanna did that though, she toweled down her breasts, Phil took another photo, she wiped over one breast and the other, she stood up and slid down her shorts, Phil sighed as she began to wipe herself, she had one leg up and was dabbing over the whole area.

"She shaves, I definitely want a piece of that," whispered Phil, as he clicked his phone for yet another photo, Sean wasn't watching any more, he wanted nothing to do with this plan. Unaware that she was being watched, she began to shower herself, using shower cream, Phil was getting more and more excited at the vision. Jordanna cleaned off the cream and stood naked before the two men, hiding above her, she went back to the changing bench and began to dress herself in smart clothes; Phil took even more pictures, at each stage of dressing. Fully dressed, Jordanna left the changing rooms, Phil and Sean allowed her to leave, waited five minutes then climbed down out of their hiding place. Jordanna came back out to the gym and went over to Gerard, he was using the shoulder press by this time, as she reached Gerard, Phil and Sean came back into the gym. Phil nudged Sean and pointed to the man on the shoulder press, he had noticed that he was talking to their target, Jordanna.

"It's that Gerry fellow, I've seen him here before, but there's something about him that rings a bell. If he gets in the way of this evening's entertainment, he'll be dead meat!" He suggested. Jordanna smiled at Gerard and started to speak to him.

"You look in pretty good shape Gerry, do you fancy going for a drink after training? If you do, I'll be at Jenny's Bar, she's a good friend," she hinted, he stopped his exercising to take the card she held out and smiled at her, there was definitely an attraction between them.

"Sure, why not, I'd love to," he answered in his soft tone.

Jordanna loved to hear him speak; she fluttered her eyelids at him and puckered her lips, then kissed the fresh air between them. Phil noticed their attraction and he wasn't happy about it at all, he stormed out of the gym to the car park. Sean ran out after him, Phil was furious and Sean tried to appease him.

"What's got in to you, why are you acting like this?" Implored Sean.

"She's mine! And that weasel isn't going to have her," seethed Phil, he started to calm down and began thinking of a plan to scupper 'Gerry'. He waited for Jordanna to leave the gym, then told Sean to follow her to see where she was going and ring him where she ended up. Sean set off with his part of the plan; at least he didn't have to do anything horrible. Phil waited for Gerard to finish his routine, which took a further forty-five minutes, much to Phil's annoyance. As he came down the steps of the gymnasium, Phil approached him and said.

"Hey friend, have you seen this girl, she's my girlfriend, and she sometimes goes here?" Showing Gerard, a dressed version on his photo gallery, he recognized Jordanna and started to worry that she was just teasing him.

"Yeah, she was in earlier but she's already left though, I'm last out," he explained.

He was concentrating on the picture of Jordanna, so hadn't noticed who the man was at first. But when he looked up, he recognized him straight away and noted a look of mischief on Phil's face and felt he should protect Jordanna from him.

"Look, I don't know where she goes after she leaves here," explained Gerard.

Just then Phil's phone rang and it was Sean, he turned his back on Gerard to take the call.

"She's at Jenny's Bar, just gone to the toilet," revealed Sean. Phil rang off without reply and faced Gerard again.

"Sorry mate, I'd love to catch up with you, but she's gone drinking with friends, so I'll have to leave you, see you around Gerry," said Phil, Gerard frowned at him, then decided to follow to see what he was up to, and tailed behind a few yards.

Sean was waiting at Jenny's for Phil to come in, he entered and bought two bottles of beer went over to Sean and handed him one.

"Boy, we are in for a good time tonight, if we get in with her!" Yelled Phil, the music was unbearably loud. Sean had sunk the first bottle very quickly and went to buy more. Gerard had followed Phil to Jenny's and sat at the back of the bar watching Phil and Sean, a cocktail waitress came over for his order, and he sent her away for a vodka and lemonade. Phil stood up from his seat and went across to Jordanna, as he approached she turned her head and smiled at him.

"Listen, I saw you at the gym earlier, I would like to buy you, and your friend a drink, if that's okay?" He asked, as his charm was working on the ladies, Jordanna wiggled on her stool.

"Sure, of course you can," she answered. "This is Jenny."

Jenny Sweetman had inherited the bar from her father and changed its name to hers. Jenny was strong and confident, pretty, with a fuller figure than Jordanna and long blonde hair. Phil waved Sean over after his initial move, he came over cautiously, Gerard was studying all of this, and he noticed that Sean wasn't very comfortable being there, looking about all the time, not interested in the women. A couple of hours later and the foursome were getting very drunk and getting along very well it seemed. Phil suggested they left for something to eat. Jenny said.

"Look I own this place and live upstairs, so I'm not going anywhere, okay boys, so see ya and goodnight."

Jenny kissed Sean on the cheek and hugged Jordanna. Jordanna was left alone with these two drunken men and she went to sit back down.

"Look, if Jenny isn't coming then I won't be going either, I don't wish to make a spare wheel out of your friend here," she said.

Jordanna was attracted to Phil a little, but not enough to offer it out on a plate to him. She went to leave, and Phil watched her walk off, their plan had failed, all those drinks he'd bought her and his full range of chat up lines wasted on this woman. He started to feel angry and went after her, Sean followed rapidly behind him fearing for her safety. Jordanna walked quickly away from Jenny's, down a small alleyway as a short cut to the main road, Phil caught up and pulled her back into the alleyway, his hand was over her mouth so she couldn't make any noise, Sean had joined him and Phil forced him to help carry Jordanna back to the car park.

"Right hold her tightly, I want a closer look at her," he ordered.

Sean did what Phil asked and held on to her, Phil knelt in front of her, he raised her skirt up, revealing her slim panties, as he held her skirt up, Phil just looked at her for a few moments.

"Look, guys don't do this okay, you seem like nice men, so please leave me?" She pleaded.

Sean covered her mouth over again, he'd held Jordanna with her arms behind her back, and Phil began to unbutton her shirt, as he did this slowly his eyes were glazing over.

"I want to taste those gorgeous titties of yours," Phil demanded, as he finished opening her top and yanked her bra cups down, her breasts came out, inches away from Phil's face.

"Look at these Sean," he said lustily, his other hand was squashing all over her, squeezing and hurting her, she could smell Phil's beer breath as he licked over her. Sean couldn't see very much from behind, just then Phil knelt back down, he pushed his thumbs up either side of her panties, he rubbed against her skin inside, Jordanna was crying and wiggling, this was exciting Phil, the way her breasts wobbled above him, he was turned on even more. Phil then slid Jordanna's panties down and sighed as her polished vagina appeared before his eyes, his right thumb stroked against it.

"Jesus, what a view," gasped Phil, and moved in closer to look at her.

"Hey you guys, what's going on here? Fucking leave her alone will you!" Gerard, had discovered them.

Phil and Sean pushed Jordanna away; she fell to the ground in her half-dressed state.

"You should have minded your own business, now we're gonna have to shut you up," threatened Phil.

He moved over to a skip and pulled out some pieces of wood, he threw a piece over to Sean, they raced at Gerard and swung at him, they hit him in the face and torso, Gerard doubled over and covered his face with his hands, in pain. Sean kicked him from behind, this fighting allowed Jordanna to correct her clothing again, she stood frozen for a moment and was appalled by what she saw next, Gerard was laying huddled on the floor, Phil and Sean were battering him with wood, kicks and punches. They rained blows down on him; time and time again they hit him. Because Gerard had been training earlier, all his muscles were stiff with lactic acid, so couldn't really defend himself.

"Stop it! Please?" She screamed.

The two men halted straight away, seemed to sober up and realize what they had done, then ran off up the alley. Jordanna ran to Gerard's side and was looking at him, his face was bloodied and bruised, a deep gash ran down his left cheek, she was thankful that he had come to her rescue, a few moments more, she may have been raped. He was breathing heavily from his beating, Jordanna helped him up, noticing he still looked quite handsome, even with cuts and bruises.

"Thank you, Gerry, you saved me, how did you find me?"

Gerard stood there, propped up by her, spat blood from his cheeks to the floor before answering.

"I knew they were up to no good, when I saw them earlier, so followed Phil to the bar where you were, but I thought I'd lost you when you all left, then I heard your voice and here I am."

"Well I'm very grateful you are here, now where do you live? Come on I'll help you get home."

"My flat's only a few blocks away, but be warned, my father's staying with me for a while, he can be a little strange," replied Gerard. They walked together to his flat and rang the intercom.

"Who is it, please?" Asked a German voice.

"I am sorry to disturb you, I have your son with me, he's been attacked," explained Jordanna.

"Very well, I am coming to assist you, wait there," Emmerich replied, he arrived at the door and opened it, Gerard fell in and collapsed on the floor, Emmerich looked at this young lady and she looked at him, his features were as handsome as Gerard's, he just looked older, the same kindness was in his eyes so she felt safe. They helped Gerard upstairs to the flat and laid him down on the sofa, Jordanna went and got warm water, a soft cloth and anti-septic, she began to clean up Gerard's injuries. He was wincing at each dab of material on his cuts; Emmerich sat watching this girl, lovingly tend to his son and then asked her. "Who did this to him, can you tell me who they are?"

She stopped her nursing and said.

"They were two men, they were trying to rape me, Gerry stopped them, they were two blokes from the bar I was in," she explained.

"Will you recognize them, if you saw them again?" He inquired. Gerard raised his head and gave out their names.

"Philip Barker and Sean Curle, they were at my school in Mortal Dean. They use the same gym as us, tonight they followed Jordanna from there," came his response.

"In that case, you are lucky my son was there to protect you," Emmerich pointed out. "Listen you must stay here, it is getting late you can use the spare bedroom, I'll sleep out here."

"Oh! Thank you, if I may, it's been a bit of an ordeal, and thanks again Gerry," she said, kissed him on the forehead, Emmerich showed her through to the bedroom. As Jordanna disappeared out of sight, Emmerich went to Gerard on the sofa and looked down at him.

"She's a beautiful girl son, are you sure about these men?" He asked and sat stroking his forehead.

Gerard nodded then Emmerich got up again, he walked into the kitchen and opened a drawer, inside was a biscuit tin, he brought this out to the sitting room and took the lid off. He sat back at the sofa and put the tin on the coffee table, he took out a few photographs, then sat Gerard up and asked him.

"If they went to your school, do you recognize them in these photographs, and would you please point them out to me?" Gerard studied them for a few seconds and then pointed out Phil and Sean's faces from a class photograph. Emmerich took the photo, then put the others back and closed the lid.

"Rest now son, I will make you something to drink," he said.

Gerard lay back and began to relax again, meanwhile, Emmerich went back to the kitchen, he quickly cut the images of Phil and Sean from the photograph, then from another cupboard, he took out the projector he had used before, then finally made some hot drinks. Emmerich went through to the spare bedroom and looked around the door, Jordanna had made herself at home and was fast asleep in the bed. His expression changed quickly, he wrestled with his thoughts and he felt sickened that two strong men had tried to rape a defenceless girl and then attacked his son, for coming to her rescue. He became angry and took the things he'd collected back into the sitting room, he placed the projector on the coffee table, switched it on and a light glowed on the far wall. The photographs were positioned ready to feed to Gerard; he saw that his son was resting, his eyes closed. He began his terrible countdown.

"Ten, nine, eight, seven, six, you are feeling completely focused." Gerard responded to Emmerich's words, his eyes snapped open. "Five, four, three, two, one, now you will complete your journey of retribution."

Emmerich clicked his fingers, Gerard was in a trance, his sores no longer hurt him, and he sat upright. Emmerich slid the pictures of Phil and Sean under the projector, Gerard's gaze fixed on them.

"Look at these men, they tried to attack your girlfriend tonight and they laughed at you when you tried to save her," he stated. "Are you going to let them get away with it, are you going to allow that to happen, they need to be taken out of existence, what if they do rape her next time?" Conditioned Emmerich. Gerard became immensely angry at his father's words, he bristled with fury, his eyes totally transfixed on the faces of Phil and Sean. "Go to them son, and send them to the hell they belong," ordered Emmerich.

Gerard got up and walked to his room, he got out his coat and scarf from his wardrobe, put these on, and he came back to the sitting room, as he stood there in his stalking clothes, Emmerich swelled with pride.

"Take it to them son, make them pay." Emmerich threw his car keys to Gerard and he snatched them from mid-air with sharpened reflexes. Out from the flat and down to the car park, he found the Land Rover, got in and drove to Mortal Dean.

It was nearly three in the morning and everywhere was quiet. A taxi pulled up next to the bus shelter, Phil and Sean flopped from the cab and staggered the few yards up the road to the house they shared. A Land Rover rolled up silently to the kerb, Gerard watched as Phil and Sean fumbled for their house keys, taking ages to get in the house and as they finally managed it, Gerard stepped out of his vehicle, opened the back and took out a hammer and a crow bar. He walked with absolute silence to the front door, put an ear to the door and listened for the two men and heard them shouting at each other.

"You went way over the top tonight Phil, nearly raping a girl, we don't do things like that, you must be on steroids of something, I've never seen you like that before and we knew the girl. We normally go for complete strangers, no come backs remember?" Sean yelled, so embarrassed by what they had done to Jordanna that his words of disgust blurted out of him. Phil looked at Sean blankly, threw his keys onto the hall table, grabbed Sean by his shirt and said.

"Listen we spent a ton of money on that girl and she didn't deliver, after her display at the gym, I just had to have a closer look at her. The fucking little show off deserved it anyway, flaunting her boobs and wiggling her arse at us and then no pay off, fuck that!" Phil pushed Sean away and they stumbled into the lounge.

"Listen Sean, you can't say anything to anybody okay, you know what happens if you do, this picture goes to my Dad," he threatened, as he showed the photo of Sean and his sister together.

"Fuck you Phil! Show him go on, that won't bother me now, after what we did tonight, we deserve to be lifted for it, so show your Dad, besides your sister loved it all anyway, so fuck yourself," Sean yelled back.

Gerard peered through the letterbox, he could see keys on the hall table and he pushed a long stick through, lifted the keys, pulled them towards him and quietly let himself in. The argument in the lounge escalated, and Gerard stood outside listening to their raised voices. Phil was getting even more agitated, Sean stood up and squared his chest to Phil.

"You deserve to go down for what you did tonight and that bloke, he was only trying to help her," reasoned Sean.

"I've remembered who that interfering idiot is; he's Outlaw, you know, Gerard Swales, the lads used to pick on him at school," Phil shouted.

"He can't be, he was such a skinny kid."

"That was Swales alright, back from the dead."

And as he said that the lounge door burst open and there he stood, the figure in the black shiny coat, the one Sean had seen from the factory window, who had threatened to slit his throat, Sean turned to run away but Gerard threw the hammer, it spun in the air, struck him on the back of his head and sent him sprawling over the armchair, knocking him out instantly, Phil lunged at Gerard but got a knee into his stomach, all the air in his chest gushed out, he was coughing and gasping, then Gerard punched him on the jaw and he fell to the floor, Gerard stood over him, he tried to kick out but Gerard grabbed his foot and twisted it quickly, it snapped with a horrid crack, he screamed and tried crawling away but Gerard moved too quickly for him and knocked him out with a rabbit punch to the back of his neck.

Gerard went back to the car and got some binding tape, he quickly bound Phil's hands and feet together, then went over to Sean and did the same with him; he carried the two men to the Land Rover. He tidied the lounge, hiding the scuffle, locked the front door of the house again then ran quickly to the car and drove to a reservoir, a few miles to the south of Mortal Dean. When he arrived Phil and Sean were still unconscious, Gerard dragged them to the edge of the purification tank that he remembered from boyhood. The water was pumped in and filled the tank to a depth of ten feet, it was then treated with fluoride and chlorine to clean it and after two hours it would be pumped out again. He would watch the five o'clock surge most evenings when he was a kid living at Brown Gale, it was one of his private places where the other kids didn't disturb him, so he knew how quickly the water would come in. It was four o'clock in the morning; he had an hour to put the two men into position. Knowing the surge was due every twelve hours helped Gerard, he carried Sean down first and held him to the stepladder and bound his body tightly to it, next he brought down Phil and carefully laid him down on the hard surface of the basin floor, he placed him in a way that his neck was in line with a metal bar shaped like a guillotine, when the timer switched the power on, this bar would fly round quickly and open the gates to let the water rush in. The idea would be that Phil would be decapitated and then Sean will drown for his own sins. Gerard finished his binding and climbed back out of the basin and stood waiting for the men to awaken. Half an hour later, Sean began to stir into consciousness; he opened his eyes and found he was upside down.

"Hey where am I, who are you? Don't hurt us please," he pleaded. Sean could see Phil further down from him, trussed up, with this machine right beside his head and began to fear for their lives. Gerard came into view; he appeared upside down and was still wearing his scarf and coat.

"You attacked a girl tonight, and the man who tried to help her, I know you have regrets about it, so I am granting you salvation to cleanse you of your sins," announced Gerard. "As for him, he is going straight to hell, and his soul will float around here for eternity," he added.

Phil was coming to and all he could see was Sean hanging upside down from a ladder,

"Hey how did we get here?" He shouted, as his eyes began to focus and a figure appeared before him, looking through Phil's phone; he found Jordanna's photos and chose the absolutely naked one taken in the showers while she wasn't looking and stared at it, he turned it round slowly to show Phil.

"She is a pretty girl, isn't she? You've captured her beauty so well, shame it will be the last time you do this," said Gerard.

He put the phone into Sean's pocket, and climbed back out again. He looked at his watch and started to count the last ten seconds to five o'clock.

"One, two, three, four, five, six, seven, eight, nine, ten," he counted.

Suddenly, as the klaxon sounded and the mechanism began to start working, he came around to his normal consciousness, his usual considerate self, unaware of what he'd just been doing. It was too late though, the bar flicked round and sliced down on to Phil's neck, taking his head clean from his body, the gate opened right out and the water gushed through, running red with Phil's blood and rose very quickly, Gerard desperately tried to save Sean, but too late, the water washed up over him and way up to the ten-foot level. Gerard fell to his knees, he had no idea how he had got there, his aches and pains had returned, and he knew something bad had happened; he pulled himself up and scrambled away from the scene as quickly as he could, feeling afraid and confused. He returned to the Land Rover and drove fast, all the way to the City, he was trying to remember how he got from laying on the couch, with cuts on his face, to watching two former school pupils dying before his very eyes. He didn't care much for Phil's predicament though he'd deserved his fate. The pains from his earlier beating, coursed through him as he drove, it was hard to control his driving. He eventually managed to get back to the flat and crept in quietly, he could see that his father was snoring on the sofa bed so he went straight to his bedroom and lay there for hours, trying to work things out. He eventually fell asleep physically drained from the night's experiences. While Gerard slept, Emmerich came into his room and counted to ten, believing it would bring him out of his trance. When Gerard woke up six hours later, he could hear Emmerich and Jordanna talking next door in the lounge, he got dressed and went to join them, Gerard was still thinking of what happened earlier, did he kill those men or did somebody else do it and had they set him up by leaving him there. He looked at Jordanna, she noticed his confusion and stood up and went over to him.

"What is it, have I done something wrong?" She asked.

Gerard shook his head, took her by the hand and led her out of the flat; he turned to Emmerich and said.

"I think it's time that I took this young lady home." His father just nodded back without a word and carried on reading his newspaper. Leading Jordanna out into the landing, Gerard held her to him and kissed her on the lips, which she responded to.

"Listen, I like you a lot and want to see you again, but right now I've got to visit someone okay," he said.

Kissing her again at length, they walked to the bus stop. Gerard held her until the bus arrived, she got on board and waved as the bus drove away out of sight.

Still at the front of his mind were the events that took place earlier at the reservoir, visions of Phil floating up without a head and the frothing red water. Sean tied upside-down, and then drowning right in front of him. He had no explanations, but with his newfound determination, needed to find some answers. He tried desperately to remember anything else, what did he do between his flat and where he awoke? Why was he wearing that coat, where did he get it? He still ached from his beating off Phil and Sean, he stopped to look at his cuts in a shop window, Jordanna had tidied them up well. The gash on his cheek was plastered, but his left eye looked blackened. Gerard decided that he would visit Michaela; she might be able to answer his questions. He started the long walk over to Michaela's house.

Chapter 12

Revelation, the Regional Serious Crime Squad Arrive.

A police car stopped outside Michaela's house; Steve stepped out and said.

"Look Paul, go to the university, find Professor Deichmann's address, pick him up and then come back here when you've finished, I'll only be an hour, then we'll go looking for Gerard Swales." Paul nodded without a word and sped away. Steve walked up to the front door and rang the gong. Franks answered and announced Steve's visit to Michaela.

"The Detective is here again Madam,"

"Show him to my study please, I'll be along in a second," she ordered.

As Franks led Steve to the now familiar study, he could hear children's voices coming from the sitting room; and whilst he stood waiting for Michaela, he looked at the photographs dotted about, one particular image stood out more than the others, it was Gerard, in this picture he was relaxed, looking confident, with kind eyes, much different to the picture he had in his drawer back at the station. Franks had made drinks at Michaela's request and brought them to the study, seconds later she entered; her hair was down and she was dressed more casually this time, her Sunday attire as she called it; Jodhpurs, with a loose fitting, light blue silk blouse tied at the waist, her perfume was very enticing.

"Sorry, I've been riding with my children this morning, so forgive the state of dress," she said, handing a whisky to Steve and sitting in her high chair again. "How can I be of assistance, it's Steve isn't it?" Michaela recalled.

Steve drank his whisky down quickly before speaking.

"I want to know if you ever treated a client called Gerard Swales, and what can you tell me about him?"

"You know that I can't discuss patients without their consent, besides he's a lovely man, who wouldn't hurt anyone," she said, defensively.

"Listen he may be involved in some nasty business, his father George Swales was killed just two days ago, so if you can help us please, now is the time," he insisted. Michaela, seeing his determination, changed her tack

"Okay, but not here, we have to go up to my office, it is more private there."

Steve agreed and followed her out to her office, he could smell the perfume again he was beginning to find her irresistible. They reached Michaela's office; she turned before opening the door.

"Steve, I must warn you before we enter, whatever happens in here, stays in here, any information I give out, you must keep to yourself, please I must insist?"

Steve nodded and allowed her to open the office door and followed her in, the sexual tension between the pair began to rise. Michaela sat at her desk and opened her filing cabinet; she took out Gerard's records and placed it open on the desk.

"Gerard Swales was an extremely sensitive teenager; when I discovered him begging on the streets, twenty years ago, I could tell he was troubled and offered him a place of shelter. He stayed here full time while I treated him, you must understand that he was completely traumatized, when he was a boy he had been bullied by other children, not the usual name calling I must add, but torture and torment and not just the children either, his own father physically and mentally abused him including using a cattle prod on him, he was left completely ostracized, very shy and bereft of confidence when he arrived here, when he finally explained what had happened to him, I had to spend a lot of time shielding this hurt from him," she continued.

"Tell me what these kids did to him then, maybe I will start to feel a little sorry for him? Because right now I don't," said Steve.

"Very well; here is a case in point, when he was fourteen years old, his manhood was severely disfigured, here is the picture." Michaela flipped the photo over to show him.

Steve took the picture, sat down and looked at it, he made a gasp at the severity of Gerard's injuries, he could see that all the way along there were second-degree burns.

"Did he tell you how this happened?" He asked, looking up at Michaela.

"He told me that he was tricked into going to a party, there he was ambushed and tied up, two girls then stripped his clothes off and tied a firework to his genitalia, from the result and extent of burns over the area, you can guess what happened next," she explained.

"They burnt the boy, for what reason, I don't understand, who were these girls?" Steve asked. Michaela stood and moved round to the front of her desk, sat at the edge of it and crossed her legs.

"Gerard gave the names of his torturers as Betty and Caitlin Jones, no other explanation was given except Betty was the girlfriend of a Luke Jarvis at the time, he may have suggested the idea to them," she revealed, Steve handed back the picture of Gerard's burns and she placed it back in the file.

"You realize that these three people are dead, and that it could be Gerard who killed them?" He reasoned.

"No not at all Steve, you see I have placed him under hypnosis and reconditioned his mind to accept it was a terrible ordeal and to confidently deal with it, move on with his life. It must be a coincidence they are dead because it couldn't be him," she reasoned.

Michaela was adamant that she had been successful in her treatment of Gerard and Steve was beginning to be affected by what the boy had been through and knew that Michaela was being honest with him, so asked.

"Is there anything else that happened, maybe you could convince me to pursue a different person?"

Michaela eased herself off her perch, walked to the cabinet and brought out a second file, she returned to her position of the end of the table and re-crossed her legs, knowing she was entertaining Steve with her tight breeches.

"Case two is a bit different to the first, four boys made his life so difficult that Gerard couldn't make any kind of friendships; they whipped him with wet towels every P.E lesson while he was naked, plus when he was fourteen, they played a game of Russian roulette with him, just because he dared to look at another boy's girlfriend, they also shot him at close range with paintball guns, these are all nasty forms of torture. He gave their names as Richard Joiner, Jeremy Stanley, Luke Jarvis and Colin Rusdale, they finally tarred and feathered him on his last days at school," she revealed. "And that, together with his father's brutality, was the final straw that made him run away from home."

Steve could feel Michaela was trying to make him kiss her, but held back and waited for her to make a move.

"Look; all these people you mentioned are also murder victims, it still points the finger at him," he argued.

"Again, you're mistaken, I have reconditioned him to help him move forward from it, not to dwell on what had happened to him, if you ask him, you will find that he has only vague memories of the traumas he suffered," she argued back.

Steve was feeling a mixture of emotions again, pleased he was getting some important facts to corroborate his case, excited by Michaela's seductiveness, and guilt as his wife slipped into his thoughts. Brenda hadn't been very loving towards Steve over recent years and she'd become increasingly paranoid about his partnership with Lana Scannell, when they had worked in the Met together. She thought they were too close for comfort, spending too much time together, so she insisted that he transfer to Mortal Dean. Michaela was showing him more attention than Brenda had lately and Steve was enjoying it. However, he still wanted to ask two more questions.

"These boys who attacked Mr Swales, they seem to have been a gang at school, and now they are being killed in some sort of order, so who else might know about Gerard's situation?"

Michaela re-crossed her legs one more time and leaned back on her desk.

"Well, there was one session that my Husband sat in on, early in the treatment when Gerard presented every case," she answered, moving from the desk and kneeling on the floor in front of Steve, his gaze fixed on her as she moved. She looked terrific and stayed kneeling for a while so he could see down the opening of her blouse and her lovely breasts under it, but still Steve didn't want to make a move without invitation.

"So… so, you think he might be influencing Gerard in some way, or could it be one of the other kids who stayed here at the time?" Steve asked, knowing what was going to come next.

"I don't think it was Emmerich who killed them, he is too kind, and the other kids here never witnessed each other's sessions, all that was kept confidential," came her final answer.

Questioning over, she stood and sat on the casting couch, making Steve sit backwards, as she moved along next to him, he was breathing in her perfume. They kissed deeply for ages, but Steve broke away from her.

"Look, Michaela, you are very tempting and believe me, you are a terrific lady and I would easily like to make love to you, but I am with Brenda and don't want to spoil what we have, just for a sneaky clinch," he said, handing back the file he'd been reading.

Michaela was the most incredible woman he had ever met, they were barely strangers but she treated him as though she'd known him all her life.

"If you do wish to come back or are having difficulties with your wife, then please call?" Michaela was still trying to tempt him as they left the office and went back down to the hall, she kissed him again. Steve smiled at her and left, she watched him walk down the driveway.

As Steve got to the end of the road, Gerard came walking up from the other end. He was walking briskly and turned up Michaela's driveway before Steve turned around. Gerard rang the gong and again Franks answered. He had grown fond of Gerard when he stayed there and was pleasantly surprised to see him standing there; after all it had been fourteen years between visits.

"Mr Swales, so good to see you, I hope you are well? Dr Deichmann will be pleased you dropped by. Just go into the library and wait one moment and I'll summon her," said a delighted Franks.

"Thanks, Derek, that would be good of you," replied Gerard, who had always remained on first name terms with Franks. The butler walked down the long hall to the sitting room, knocked and entered, Michaela was watching her daughters playing before her, she looked at Franks and said.

"Another visitor, Franks? My I am a popular soul today, aren't I?"

"It's Mr Swales, Doctor, he's in the library."

Her eyebrows rose at Gerard's mention, she got up from her chair and went to her study without a word; Franks remained with the children. As Michaela stepped into the room, she could see Gerard was troubled; she invited him to sit and sat in her therapy chair.

"You look perplexed Gerard, what can I do to ease that?" She asked professionally.

"I think I've done something bad, but I can't remember doing it. There are these moments over the last few weeks, where my memory is totally blank. Then earlier this morning, I sort of 'came to' down at the old Mortal Dean reservoir and I watched two men die, I don't know how I got there, whether I killed them or if somebody put me there to frame me," he revealed.

"That is a tricky situation you've got yourself into, how can I help?" She asked.

"Could you please try and regress me again, help me remember the bits that I can't, see how far back it goes and who did this to me, please? I am going out of my mind here," he pleaded.

"Okay Gerard relax, of course I'll do as you ask, but Franks will be in attendance in case you should get aggressive and attack me, have you got that?" Explained Michaela, he nodded.

She made him stay in the library whilst she explained to Franks what was about to occur. Franks went to get his Berretta from his quarters and then followed Michaela back in; she guided him over and drew the black curtains around the bay windows.

"Right, remain here please Franks? If Gerard makes any aggressive moves towards me, you are here to protect me without condition, understand?" She instructed.

With a bow of his head, Franks agreed, he had done this before, so she knew he would be reliable. Michaela disappeared to collect Gerard and returned moments later, led him to the casting couch and asked him to lie down and make himself comfortable. At first Michaela put on some meditation music, soft chiming and water lapping on the shore, this reminder of his years of therapy made Gerard relax straight away. Michaela moved to her normal position behind the top of Gerard's head, sat on the chair and leaned forward; she rubbed her hands together briskly and placed both hands on his forehead. The heat from her hands seemed to soothe Gerard even more, and then she began to speak softly to him.

"I will count from ten, and as I do this you will begin to look back over the last few weeks in stages, at every number that I count, you will explain to me what point you've reached and what is going on, nod your head twice if you understand?" Instructed Michaela. Gerard nodded twice and she began.

"Ten, where are you now?" She questioned, Gerard opened his eyes and could see he was in his Father's flat.

"I'm at home, looking at a photo of two men, they are smiling," he answered.

"How does this make you feel?" She probed.

"Angry, they tried to rape Jordanna and they hurt me for saving her, I really want to hurt them back, but the pain is stopping me," he replied, she made a brief note then carried on with the process.

"Remember what did you do to these people? Where did you take them?"

Gerard was staring upwards and slowly gave his answer.

"I tied them up with strong tape, Barker is laying on the floor, he is going to have his head cut off for trying to hurt Jordanna and Curle will drown for playing his part in it."

Michaela could see he was getting agitated at what he was saying but allowed him to complete the episode.

"Nine, where are you now Gerard?" She said.

"I am on the farm where my mother lives, standing in front of George, he's wet and angry, but I don't care because I am angrier," he growled.

"Why are you there, who sent you, what happened next?" She coaxed.

"I want to ask some questions, why did he hurt me, how was I different to my brother and sister, Father sent me, said he should be punished for hurting me, so I punished him, fried his arse and watched him die!" Gerard scowled as he spoke.

Michaela was shocked at this revelation, now she knew Emmerich was involved somehow. She counted to the next number.

"Eight, please tell me where you are and what is going on?" She asked, half afraid of what was coming up.

"I am in a dark room, but I can see, there is Colin stood before me, I went to school with the jerk. I hate him, he was a bully, so I cut his throat; he bled like a pig before me. There is banging on the door, two wankers from the paintball centre, I stuck an axe into Stuart and stabbed Zach four times, teach him to try and fight me," snarled Gerard.

Michaela was startled by this cool recollection, how did he not know this? Emmerich must have shielded it from him. She continued regardless, hardly believing the anger and language coming from Gerard but keen to see how far back he could remember.

"Seven, tell me Gerard what do you see, where are you now?" She inquired. His eyes flicked around as he slipped back further and then spoke.

"I am driving a lorry, that tosser Jez is driving towards me, I hate him too, I slam the lorry into him and sent him back up the road, his cocky face twisted with fright, then Bam! Over he goes, rolling over and over, I stop and get out, I need to check that he is dead, I feel good, because he deserved to die!"

"Six, what can you tell me now please Gerard?" She asked, remembering what Steve had told her about the four men being taken out in order of popularity...

"I am on a roof and that bastard Luke Jarvis is looking at me, his smarmy face gawping with surprise, I pick him up and chuck him in the cement down below, he isn't so smarmy anymore. He's asking why I'm doing this, so I tell him and show him the photo that Father gave me. I pour the cement over him and watch him choke on it, good riddance I say."

Again, he'd mentioned Emmerich. She was sure now that he was behind it all, she had forgotten about Franks, hiding behind the curtain, who coughed gently to attract her attention.

"Please excuse me Doctor, but the Professor once asked me to distract you during one of your sessions with the young man," he revealed.

"Aye, I remember, a bogus phone call, that must have been when he hid his message, how callous and typically clever, thank you Franks." He nodded and returned to his hiding place, allowing her to continue. She placed her hands back on Gerard's forehead and counted.

"Five, tell me where you are now, how did you get there and what happened?" Gerard's eyes widened and he began to speak.

"I am with Father, we are waiting in the woods for Major Richard, 'I'm God,' Joiner to run past, he's as predictable as day break, wham, we hit him and drag him to the paintball place. Father is helping me tie him down and putting the shotgun between his legs, I am tying the trigger back, Father is placing the cross bow behind him, he has taped a recording and left it for me to play as we leave. Joiner will wake to find he is helpless, but I don't stay too long to watch, we hear the bang as we leave, another piece of shit exterminated!"

Michaela knew the rest, she was furious with Emmerich for using her that way. She decided to finish this session and layer in some suggestions of her own, she needed Gerard to reveal any other killings first and then use the rest of the countdown to place a message in.

"Four, please tell me where you are Gerard, who is it you are after?" She asked. He focused on the far wall, and replied.

"I am seeing a photo of Betty and Caitlin, they are laughing at me, I feel bitter and want to hurt them like they've hurt me, Father has given me some tools to help, I am driving to Mortal Dean and I feel very cross, I have to take them out. I put some hay in the place where they trapped me before and wait for them, they arrive early and call out, I am waiting upstairs for them, they are so stupid and trap themselves in, I gave a sporting chance to escape but stupid Caitlin kicked the peg over. The rest was easy, gas them and tie them up, same as they did with me. I burn them, with fireworks to start the fire, to take away their nastiness, so they can't hurt anyone else. I don't stay but watch the flames take hold from the Land Rover, before I drive off."

He sounded so cool about it, like it was a natural thing to do. Michaela now knew the full extent of Gerard's rampage, all those people dead, because of him. To finish off the session; she continued the countdown.

"Three, thank you for your account of events that have taken place, when you awaken you will remember what you've done. Two, you won't be angry anymore or feel guilty; the man who must pay for this is your Father. One, please wake and take this knowledge with you, Emmerich must not be allowed to use you this way anymore." Her message was placed and Gerard woke, his memory was clear and everything was there at the fore.

"I can't believe Father did that to me, I didn't want those people dead, but it's too late, I must go to him and make him confess to the police."

Michaela nodded and helped him up from the casting couch; Franks came from behind the curtain, looking shocked by the revelations and relieved that the session hadn't required his intervention.

"If you need any assistance please call me, I will come at once," he offered, before leaving the office and going about his usual duties. Michaela escorted Gerard downstairs and in the hall, she turned before seeing him out.

"Now you know what happened, I hope you can resolve this, the police will be looking for you so please be careful, you know how resourceful Emmerich can be," she reminded, he kissed her left cheek before leaving and said.

"I am glad that I met you Michaela, thank you for all you've done for me and I am sorry that you heard all that up there, I can't believe all those things I've done."

"Whatever goes on up there in that office stays there?" She replied, he smiled and left the house in a hurry to have it out with his father.

Meanwhile, Paul had pulled up outside Emmerich's apartment block, he stepped out and walked to the front doors and checked the names on the letterboxes, and Emmerich's name was on number eight. Paul went in and found the door corresponding to Emmerich's letterbox, he knocked on the door and Emmerich answered it.

"Professor Emmerich Deichmann? I am Sergeant Paul Collison of Mortal Dean Police. I need you to accompany me to Mortal Dean station please," requested Paul.

"Most certainly Sergeant, let me arrange my outdoor attire," Emmerich seemed to be expecting this visit, he returned dressed in his overcoat, locked the door and accompanied Paul to his car. Paul put him in the back of the car; then proceeded to pick up Steve from the end of Michaela's road. Twenty minutes passed; as Steve waited for Paul to come back, he stared back at Michaela's house, he wanted more time with her but his instinct knew that wouldn't ever happen again. Just then Paul pulled alongside the kerb, Steve could see Emmerich sitting in the back and was pleased he had collected him without a hitch.

"This is Detective Speed, Professor, he's just been to enquire about a client of your Wife's," explained Paul.

"I think he was after more than that, right Detective?" Probed Emmerich smelling his wife's perfume, "don't worry, our marriage was destroyed by me long ago, she can do as she pleases." Steve realized he had nothing to worry about, but Paul looked at Steve a little confused.

"Never mind, it's just banter," said Steve, fending off his enquiring mind.

Paul started the car and drove to Mortal Dean. When they arrived at the police station, they noticed several cars parked up, not all of them squad cars either. One in particular, is familiar, a green Daimler belonging to Steve's old partner Detective Sergeant Lana Scannell, both officers looked at one another as Paul said.

"Looks like the cavalry have arrived."

"The Serious Crime Squad, as usual, turning up just as we've almost cracked it." Steve added sadly.

As they made their way into the station, there was a hive of activity going on, Simon looked stressed out by it all. They handed over Emmerich to Simon who escorted him to an interview room. Steve went to his office, as he entered all the people stopped talking and stared at him. The first person to speak was his old boss, DCI Kenny Purchase, and at sixty, is looking forward to retirement and very old school in his policing.

"Steve, I don't know what's been going on down here, but it needs to be sorted asap!" Putting his arm around Steve's shoulder he walked him over to the team of officers.

"Let me introduce you to the new team who are going to solve this, over here is DI Darren Lane, the criminal profiler, he'll determine the mind set of this individual, and why he is doing this. Secondly you know your old partner, DS Scannell, she will be giving assistance while you interview any suspects, and finally this is Dr Sandra Henderson, Psychologist, who will try and get this nutter tracked down, she will take instruction from Sergeant Collison. So far there's been nine murders, a record in this region and now it seems that there's been two more, while you were out, a call came in, we've sent DC Pete Wilson our young scene of crime specialist to accompany Shabby Stores to check it out. This has gone too far Steve and we are here to prevent it getting even more out of hand," revealed the DCI.

"Thank you, Sir, but we're beginning to tie up loose ends around here, in fact I've learned some fresh information this morning and have brought in a suspect for questioning, a Professor Deichmann," assured Steve.

He didn't want the kudos of solving this case going to the SCS glory boys, so decided he would keep some information back for himself.

"Very well then Steve, get in there and question him, Lana, join him, would you?" The DCI ordered. She nodded with acceptance and followed Steve to the Interview Room holding Emmerich.

"It's been a while Steve, since we last worked together I mean, let's hope your wife isn't still jealous hey," said Lana.

"Look Sarge, the past is this past okay, and I am well over all that, we might have had a thing between us, but we never followed it up, Bren felt threatened and I am lucky that we didn't end up where we were heading, I am not really enjoying myself here alright," replied Steve.

Lana just shrugged his hand away and walked into the interview room and they sat opposite Emmerich, who didn't seem at all worried about why he was there. Steve began the interview, by saying.

"You know who I am, DC Steve Speed and this is DS Lana Scannel. We are making enquiries about a series of murders in Mortal Dean, I would like to begin by asking where you have been, over the last two and a half weeks?"

Emmerich raised his head and gave his answer.

"I have been on a hunting holiday, with my friends from University, we spent two weeks in an isolated cabin and since my return I have been preparing classes for my students."

Steve wrote this down on his notepaper and then asked.

"Can you explain to us then Professor, how two weapons bought by your Wife on your behalf, have ended up in our forensics lab, linked to the murder of Major Richard Joiner?"

Emmerich remained emotionless.

"They were stolen, we went for a walk one day, we had locked the cabin up and went on a long hike, we returned to find the window broken and the weapons were gone, go over there and look for yourself," said Emmerich calmly.

"Who else was with you while on holiday? We will need to question them, so please give us names?" Lana asked.

"Myself, briefly a man named Saul Reading, and Gerard Swales," he answered, confidently knowing Gerard wouldn't remember anything and Saul had been primed with what to say in any eventuality.

Steve's ears pricked up at the name of Gerard Swales. He prepared to question Emmerich on the subject.

"Gerard Swales' name keeps popping up in our enquiries Professor, can you tell me the relationship between you and this man?" Steve asked.

"Gerard was a client of my wife's, she counseled him after a few childhood traumas, we kind of liked each other's company, so I took him hunting with us, if you want to question him, then bring Gerard in here and let me go," replied the Professor.

"Well two days ago, his father George was found dead at his farm, brutally electrocuted, we need to find him to tell him and ask him some questions," said Steve.

Emmerich showed no reaction, to the surprise name thrown in by Steve.

"Gerard lives in the City now. But you won't find him at home right now," he explained.

"One final question then before you can go, will you please confirm, that you did not murder Betty and Caitlin Jones, Richard Joiner, Jeremy Stanley and Luke Jarvis?" Asked Lana.

"I can categorically say, that I did not kill those people, and if you think that I did, then that is something you need to prove, what an absurd thing to suggest, because quite clearly you have no evidence to back it up, and nothing to substantiate that I did," answered Emmerich; he knew they were chasing shadows.

"Very well Professor, we will let you go, while we investigate your claims, but don't go far, we will be speaking to you again shortly I'm sure," said Steve.

"Thank you, Detective, I'll be at my flat or giving a lecture at the university," said Emmerich, however he had a feeling that Steve knew more than he was letting on, he decided he would have to try and derail

Steve's investigation. After letting him go, Steve and Lana returned to the main office.

"Well, anything from him?" Asked Kenny.

"I'm certain that he knows far more than he's saying, but until we get our hands on this Gerard Swales, we can't tie him down." Steve replied. Paul was looking sadly over at Steve; he already knew what was coming.

"No Steve I'm sorry, you are officially removed from this case as of today, you're tired and worn out mate, why don't you have a few days off and recharge yourself? Then you can come back in," ordered Kenny.

Steve was disappointed by the lack of faith from his former boss, but went to his desk anyway and collected a few things. He stared at the incident board, the whole area was covered in pictures and theories, and he was going to find Gerard ahead of these bullying cretins from the SC squad. Before leaving for home, Steve locked his desk and picked up his photo of Rita. Lara looked over his shoulder.

"My, hasn't she grown; isn't it her birthday soon, this'll give you time to set up a party for her, send her my regards won't you?" She slapped him on the shoulder and grinned.

Steve's thoughts immediately switched to Rita, he had completely forgotten, her thirtieth birthday was on Tuesday. Paul didn't think Steve had been treated fairly by the DCI, so before Steve left, he handed him a piece of paper, on it was his mobile phone number. As he shook his hand the paper was exchanged.

"Listen if anything comes up, I'll tell you straight away, we won't shut you out entirely," said Paul.

"Just don't let the DCI play Sheriff and his deputies with you. I know you would hate that, anyway he was probably right a couple of days off would do me some good," replied Steve, deciding to take this opportunity to arrange a surprise party for Rita.

He went home immediately, to discuss his plans with Brenda, who was more than delighted with his help, she had the main parts of it sorted out already so she gave him the job of ringing around inviting all the family.

Chapter 13

Rita's Birthday Party.

Gerard reached his father's apartment and let himself in when he didn't get an answer, he looked around for any materials he could use, just in case Emmerich tried to entrance him again. He found a hair brush in his father's bedroom, on it were a couple of grey hairs, before picking them off, Gerard went back to the kitchen, found the first aid box and took out some surgical gloves, he put these on, then returned to Emmerich's room, he picked up the hair brush and carefully put a few hairs into a small clear plastic bag, then on the spur of the moment, opened the wardrobe and took out the Gucci travelling case his father always used and put the hair inside. He walked to the bathroom, searching for any objects Emmerich may have touched, in the waste paper bin by the bath was an old pair of latex gloves, these would be ideal, his finger prints would be on the inside, he took them and placed them in the case then continued his search, he found the keys to the Land Rover sitting on the coffee table; he picked them up, left the apartment, walked down to the carport, got in and drove round to his own flat. As he walked in the telephone rang, making him jump. He didn't pick it up and the answer machine began to work; the voice was Emmerich's.

"Son, thanks a million for your hospitality, it was a great holiday but I've had to move back to my own place, the police are asking silly questions about those killings out at Mortal Dean, they want me to stay available while they conduct their inquiries and I want to keep you out of it if possible. Oh! Another thing, I would appreciate it if you could say that the crossbow and shotgun were stolen from the cabin whilst we were hunting. Apparently, they have been detained by Forensics and they are trying to fit us up for something, they must have got to Michaela, how else would they know these were ours? I feel it would not be too long before they come to question you son, well that's it, take good care of yourself."

The answer machine stopped playing, it's usual three beeps sounded and it halted. Gerard went over to the telephone, rewound the message and replaced the tape, putting the original in another plastic bag, next he took the stalking gear from his wardrobe and packed it, along with the items he'd collected, into the Gucci case, left the flat, got in the Land Rover and hid the case with its damming evidence under an old coat in the back; before starting the car, he had a quiet smile to himself, then set off to Mortal Dean to meet up with Jordanna, who had already left two messages on his mobile phone, inviting him to join her.

After Emmerich had left his message for Gerard, he started to put his own plans into motion; he'd overheard Steve's colleagues remind him of his daughter's birthday just as he was leaving the station and thought if he could set some sort of trap for the nosy Detective, it would keep him off the case for a few weeks. He'd hired a car from the local garage and followed Steve to his house and watched as he parked the Mercedes and went inside. Brenda was still wearing her housecoat and fine-tuning the housework for the party. Steve walked up to her from behind and cuddled her; she stayed still, allowing Steve a piece of solace with her.

"They've bloody suspended me Bren, laid me off, right when I was getting along with it, I've nearly solved this bloody case, it isn't sodding fair, darling, dammit!" He cursed and banged the palm of his hand on the counter in frustration.

Brenda could smell perfume; she moved away, sat on a chair at the kitchen table, crossed her arms and wanted to know more.

"Why have you got some other woman's perfume on you? It isn't one of mine, have you been seeing somebody?"

Steve remembered his meeting with Michaela and began tactfully selecting pieces to sanitize their meeting.

"I had to visit a woman who had been treating a suspect of ours with Psychotherapy, she became a bit too seductive for my liking, she even tried to kiss me, I brushed her off though and she backed down," he explained.

Brenda seemed to accept his explanation; she had got it all wrong about him before and knew how easily a woman could fall for Steve; she did all those years ago, he was a lovely man, kind, gentle, masterful and reliable, she felt safe and secure with him.

"I am sorry you've been suspended, but at least that means that now we can concentrate on getting things in ready for Rita's party," she said, just as Steve returned from the kitchen with a beer, he knew by her hinting that she wanted to be driven somewhere, so he put the can back in the fridge.

"When you are ready, give me a shout and I will take you wherever you want to go," Steve offered.

Brenda finished off her last piece of polishing, went upstairs to their bedroom and changed clothes ready to go out. Steve swung his car keys around his fore finger, waiting for her to reappear. She came downstairs dressed in a lacy shirt with skin tight light blue flannel trousers, Steve was impressed but placed the lustful thought of making love with her to the back of his mind; he would wait for her to take the initiative.

"Come on then let's go, where would you like to go first?" Steve asked. Brenda picked up her handbag and as she walked past, leaned forward and kissed him full on the lips, she pulled back and smiled at him, then said.

"You can take me anywhere you want to, I am sorry for not always being as loving like I should be, from now on we will be a normal husband and wife." This was all music to Steve's ears; he had longed for this moment, but decided to put it on hold until later in the evening.

"I meant which shops would you like to visit? Not the other thing," he explained.

"Hypermarket first to buy food and drink, some treats for the children and, as your brother will be coming, we need to cater for his fussiness," requested Brenda.

She's walking in front of him so that he could look at her shapely backside, encased in the trousers she had chosen specially. The pair of them left the house and locked up, they walked arm in arm to the car, this was the closest they've been for years and Steve was enjoying it. Emmerich was still parked outside in the street and was pleased to see them come out rather quickly; he hated waiting around for people. He allowed them to get in and drive off before following, Emmerich wanted to see where they would end up, he let one car get in between his and Steve's, providing more cover.

As the convoy left Mortal Dean, Gerard arrived in the Land Rover; he parked in the Tug Boat car park having decided to walk to meet Jordanna, he quickly texted her phone, letting her know he was in the village, she responded and arranged to meet at the end of her road. As he approached, he could see Jordanna walking out, she stopped and waited for Gerard to reach her. She was dressed in a white leather cat suit; she looked stunning with her shiny brunette hair plaited in a long tail, draped down her back. Gerard began to breathe very heavily; he couldn't believe this was the same woman from the other night. As he reached Jordanna she smiled broadly at him. Fifteen years between them meant nothing she didn't care, if she liked the man, she would have him, regardless of how old he was. Jordanna kissed Gerard deeply when they did reach each other, her tongue darted in his mouth, Gerard responded with his own tongue, there was only one thing on her mind...

"I am so glad that I met you Gerry, if you like we could go for a walk to the woods, we would be able to spend a bit of time together there," she suggested, willing Gerard to do anything he wanted with her, after all he saved her the other night and she wanted to show her appreciation.

"Sure, I would love to walk with you, we have plenty of time to share," he replied.

Gerard was a lot more innocent than Jordanna, he didn't realize her motives for walking in these woods, but went along with her anyway. They strolled together for an hour, down winding paths and between fir trees, the pair of them holding hands all the while; they stopped on occasion to kiss each other. All this was getting too much for Jordanna; she wanted more than this and led him through a densely, overgrown piece of shrubbery. Trees surrounded the whole area; nobody could see them from the footpath, she stood Gerard against a tall tree and asked him a question.

"The other night when you saved me, did you see parts of my body at all, from where you were standing?"

"I didn't see anything, Phil was stood in the way, it was too dark to see, anyway I would ask you first, if you could show me."

"Then I want to thank you properly for saving me," offered Jordanna.

She kissed him again, this time more sensually and deeper than she'd ever done before. Gerard responded by kissing her back and lifted his hands to her breasts and caressed them from the outside of the cat suit. She kissed him slowly and with her left hand moved down to his groin, she felt him outside his trousers first, he was already stiff from their kissing. She sighed as she rubbed it for a moment and then with her thumb lowered the zip on his jeans half an inch, she slipped her fingers in and found his shorts and unbuttoned one button, she wanted to feel him, before seeing, so she could guess his size. With two fingers, she found the head of his penis through his trousers, Jordanna bit her lip as she felt him, his caressing became more purposeful around her breasts. Jordanna deftly slipped his foreskin down; his wet helmet excited her touch even more. Jordanna closed her eyes and continued to unzip Gerard; he was still caressing her body, making his penis swell a lot more. Jordanna stopped kissing to open Gerard's trousers fully, easing both thumbs into his shorts and gently lowering his trousers, she still had her eyes closed, as she was doing this, Gerard's penis bounded out of his shorts and stiffened even more in the fresh air, he had completely forgotten about his scarring. Jordanna held his penis in her hands for a few moments and then she opened her eyes, she gasped at the severity of his burns.

"Oh god! My poor Gerry, that looks really nasty, how did it happen?"

Gerard, ashamedly, quickly pulled his trousers back up and tidied himself; the magic of the moment lost forever.

"I was burnt when I was a kid, two girls hung me up and tied a firework to it, they scarred me, and I've been like this ever since, so whatever you've got planned isn't going to happen," revealed Gerard disappointedly.

Jordanna wasn't put off by his injuries, she wanted to have sex with him, but she knew it would have to wait for him to feel right and couldn't force him.

"You do know that I don't care what it looks like, I am interested in how you use it, but if you aren't ready to do this yet, then I understand."

She held his hand again, as they made their way out of the woods and back to Jordanna's house, she was feeling a little frustrated, but hoped there would be other times. As they walked up the driveway to her house, her mother was in the front garden, she took one look at Gerard and came racing over and she stood between him and Jordanna.

"Jordie, go into the house please, this is the man who killed our Jeremy, get away from him and go indoors now, keep away from us you, HELP! HELP!" Helen began screaming hoping someone would hear.

Jordanna looked back helplessly at Gerard as he sprinted off up the road. She knew that he had only been nice; maybe Mum had got it wrong.

Jordanna secretly hoped she would see him again and finish what they started in the woods. Gerard returned to the Land Rover and sat for a while, before sending a text message to Jordanna. (Sorry to cause u trouble, 1 day I hope 2 explain, I understand if you don't want me anymore). He finished sending the message, tried Emmerich with no success and then sent him a text asking where he was, he started the engine and drove off but the stress of the last couple of days started to get the better of him, so he pulled into a secluded lay-by and settled back for a sleep.

Emmerich meanwhile had followed Steve and Brenda to the supermarket, watched them sort out their parking and walk away to the store, he got out and followed behind discretely. They had a big list of things to buy, picking up wines and spirits, buffet food and canapés, but one thing they choose stood out more than most, it was a Spanish party piñata, orange in colour, the size of a small lap dog and filled with small presents to be broken open as the highlight of the party; this gave Emmerich food for thought as he formulated an idea about how he could use this. The Speeds ended their shopping spree and returned to the car park to load their car. Emmerich left them to organize his ruthless plan and drove back to the University. When he reached the University, he went to find Saul, his trusted friend. He found him walking across the quadrangle and took him to one side to ask him a favour.

"Saul my friend, I need you to come with me to the Chemistry Department, we need to procure some materials, which can help me get a monkey off my back, will you help?"

"O.K. I will help you, but this will be the last time, that business with hiring the cement lorry has really put the wind up me. I've resigned from my post, and I'm off back home to Yorkshire at the end of this semester," said Saul.

"Very well, the last time then, we must hurry, we've only a day and a half to finish this," said Emmerich, urgently, leading the way to the chemistry labs. Once there Emmerich studied all the different bottles of acids and picked out the one labeled 'sulphuric' Emmerich explained what he had planned:

"Right, we need to put some of this Sulphuric acid into a small glass tube, seal with a rubber bung, then disguise it as a sweet and hide in a piñata. So, when the piñata is hit hard; the glass will shatter, allowing the acid to fall on the victim and burn them, effectively putting this person out of the game." Saul brought around a selection of vials for Emmerich who nodded and began to set up his apparatus.

"Who's the target?" Asked Saul. Emmerich frowned and answered.

"Never mind about the name, just do this one last thing, besides you will be gone in a week and the less you know, the better."

Noticing the scalding tone in his mentor's voice, made Saul go quiet, he put on some industrial gloves and goggles; ready to pour the acid. With some tongs, Emmerich gripped the test tube, holding it steady as Saul poured the acid in, the tube filled to the top and then Emmerich placed on the rubber bung. As Saul moved the bottle away, a small drip fell on the desk and the acid burnt into the wood, sizzling away, Emmerich poured a beaker of water over it, the diluted acid smoked for a bit leaving the wooden bench scorched. The two men finished their activities and left the lab, Emmerich was pleased with this idea. He turned to Saul knowing this was the last time he'd see him and said.

"You've been a loyal friend and thank you for this, I'll keep you in the clear as my part of the bargain. I hope you find success in the future." The two men shook hands and went their separate ways, Emmerich returned to the hire car and drove back to his apartment.

Steve and Brenda had returned home and began organizing the party; Steve was tasked with phoning friends and family, making sure they knew the arrangements. Brenda started with the decorations, she wanted most of the entertainment set in the garden, and they focused on making it look inviting. At the centre was a large steel gazebo; they lined up two tables underneath it, parallel to each other. They would place the buffet on this when it was ready, with all the props in place; they called it a day and got ready for bed. Steve was still hoping for a night of passion with his wife, so when she came to the bedroom still dressed in her lacy top and trousers, he wanted to be the one to take it all off for her, with that he walked over and began to undo her top, reaching around the back to release the catch. Brenda held her arms up, allowing Steve to raise the top over her head.

"I've waited ages, are you sure you don't mind?" He asked, while she undid her trousers and pulled them down.

"Don't be silly, I'm certainly not stopping you!"

Steve picked her up in his arms and carried her over to the bed and laid her down, still in her underwear. Steve undressed quickly and was naked before she was. This often happened, seeing Steve naked made Brenda's desire the more prevalent. He was a well-endowed man, and she always marveled at his size. Steve wasted little time with removing her bra and pants before they pulled the sheets over themselves and began a night of prolonged passion.

When Emmerich got home, he noticed two missed calls; he was in no mood to be hurried, he would call them back after fixing a drink, he put the materials he'd prepared in the top drawer of his bureau, poured himself half a tumbler of Jack Daniels, then scooped up his mobile and sat back in his favourite chair; he saw the top number was Gerard's; he drank some of his JD and called him back. The ring tone made Gerard wake from his nap; he saw it was Emmerich.

"At last, where are you? Jordanna's mum is saying that I killed her son, Jeremy. I need to speak to you." Gerard's tone was urgent and irrational.

"Please try and relax, I'm at home, come over and we'll discuss it?"

Gerard immediately started the Land Rover and drove to town, his father met him at the door, ushered him into the lounge, sat him down, thrust a drink into his hand, before relaxing again in his chair.

"Tell me, who is this woman, why does she think you killed her son?" He asked.

"Remember Jordanna, the girl I rescued, well it turns out she is the little sister of Jeremy Stanley, who I went to school with, he's one of the murder victims, someone has said something because soon as she saw me, her mother started screamed at me, saying I killed him, I don't remember anything about it, so I just ran," explained Gerard, hoping that this pretence would get some information from his father; Emmerich's eyebrows rose at this revelation, he was secretly relieved Gerard didn't remember or so he thought.

"Look you've had a shock, she couldn't have known who you are, otherwise the police would have caught up with you by now, I think you should calm down and we will solve this in the morning, get some sleep," instructed Emmerich.

This wasn't what Gerard wanted, but he obeyed his father's wishes, he knew Emmerich was hiding all this from him, he wanted to know all of it, but not now and he made himself comfortable before getting to sleep.

The following morning came along very quickly. Gerard rose and waited for his father to stir; he was determined to get the answers he was seeking. Emmerich woke to the smell of coffee being poured and came down to the kitchen.

"So, tell me, does Jordanna hate you after her mother's revelation?"

Gerard took a few sips of his coffee before answering.

"I think she was more put off by my injuries, much more than her mother's screaming, she tried it on with me in the woods yesterday but because of my scars it felt awkward between us. I've left messages on her phone and I'll wait for her to contact me."

Emmerich nodded and gave advice.

"I think that is wise, she seems important to you, just try and be patient, if it is meant to be she will come to you."

Gerard was happy with this exchange, and felt he should ask more searching questions.

"I want to know if at any time, you have made me do something bad, then wiped it from my memory."

Emmerich shuffled in his chair and slurped his coffee; he was more than a little perturbed by this.

"Why would you think that of me, you are my son, I am trying to reconnect with you, and it isn't easy, finding out halfway through your lifetime, you have a child that you weren't even aware of," pleaded Emmerich.

"Well, sometimes when I have spent time with you, I ache all over, as if I've been fighting with people, and that last time, at the reservoir, when I seemed to wake up in the middle of things, I didn't know whether I had killed those two men, or if I was set up," explained Gerard. This was a big surprise for Emmerich and he shuffled uneasily.

"Don't you think maybe this was all a dream, people do have waking nightmares, you remember this yourself if I recall, and nothing about bodies in any reservoir has been reported in the news," reasoned Emmerich, trying to throw Gerard. This sort of made sense, so Gerard backed off.

"Yeah! Maybe you're right, sorry, I am just a little confused, just ignore me then," he said.

Emmerich was pleased his son's quizzing was finished.

"Listen, go to the newsagents and buy my paper, would you?" Asked Emmerich, trying to get himself a moment to set up his plan. Gerard nodded and left the flat.

Over at the Speed household things were being put into place, the finishing touches to the party were nearly there, they knew Rita would be working until three o'clock, so they had plenty of time to sort out the guests, Steve had hung the orange piñata up in the middle of the steel gazebo. This was filled with sweets and small toys, most of his family had small children, from Spanish tradition, every party ended with the breaking of a piñata. Brenda was flying around the place; she had a spring in her step following the previous evening's activities. Steve was also on his toes, they were back on track and nothing could be better.

Gerard had returned to Emmerich's apartment with the newspaper, he put the paper on the sofa and gave the change back to Emmerich who tossed it into a dish on the bureau; he then drank the rest of his coffee and went to his room to get dressed. On his return, he suddenly began counting down from ten, as he reached five, Gerard began to feel sluggish and sat down in the chair. Emmerich counted on down and by the count of one, Gerard was again completely under, Emmerich continued: The trance was weak, but working.

"You have one more task to perform for me son, and with my help you will achieve it, but not to kill anyone, just to remind somebody that he is too close to the truth and needs to back off. Do not worry, I'll be with you to guide you all the way," he took the vial of acid, nicely wrapped as a Cadbury's Flake from the drawer and showed it to Gerard. "This is what I want you to do, I will drive you to Detective Speed's house, where you will plant this into the piñata, which will probably be hanging in the garden, you then return to the car," instructed Emmerich, and Gerard nodded. "Now let's go and start our work," said Emmerich.

Back at Steve's house some of the guests were arriving, some of Brenda's sisters had flown over from Spain, her older sister Carolina and younger sister Selena. The very youngest sister, Antonia, was about to have a baby, so Brenda's parents Maria and Jose remained in Santander. Steve's brother, Brian was given the job of picking Rita up from work and bringing her over to Mortal Dean. She had no idea what was going on, she just thought her mother and father had planned a meal with her. Other guests were there; including the Stanleys, who had popped round for a small drink and everyone was waiting for Rita to arrive.

Emmerich drove Gerard to the Speed's and parked just past the house, and he waited while Gerard got out to set the trap. Gerard crept into the neighbouring garden and waited, listening by the fence, he poked his head over and scanned around, there in the middle was the gazebo with the orange piñata hanging in the centre. He checked for people before climbing over the fence and hurried quickly to the gazebo, he held the piñata and unzipped it, then poked the 'sweet' up into its belly, zipped it up and jumped away, back into the neighbour's garden and hid. The guests started to file out into the garden, they all stood waiting for the guest of honour.

It was 3:30 in the afternoon and Brian's car was coming into the street, Steve had been sent the message that they were imminent. Steve told everyone to be quiet and joined his wife in the house to greet his daughter. Emmerich was still waiting for Gerard to return, as Brian drove past him, they looked at each other; Emmerich felt uncomfortable and started the Land Rover ready to drive away quickly. Brian let Rita out of the car and they walked to the front door. Two kissing faces of her mother and father greeted Rita.

"Happy Birthday to our lovely girl. Come on in and have a drink with us!"

Rita walked between them arms around each other and walked towards the garden.

"SURPRISE!" everyone shouted. Rita was amazed to see all her Cousins, Aunties and Uncles, and Jez's family waiting there too.

"Oh! Mum, Dad thank you very much, you've gone to all this trouble for me," she said with utter joy.

"Nothing is too much trouble for our lovely girl, now come on everyone let's have a party, that's what we're here for," shouted Steve.

With that instruction the party began, children raced around the garden playing games, the adults were drinking, enjoying the fresh air and food. The party was in full swing and Gerard remained where he was, hiding behind the fence. Rita's party was heightening, the buffet was received well by both children and grown-ups. The alcohol was flowing and people were getting very tipsy, then Steve turned to everybody, so he could make a speech.

"Quiet every one, I just want to say a few words about our daughter, then we'll break the piñata. These last thirty years have been the most important time of my life, we couldn't have raised a more perfect daughter, so everyone lift their glasses for our Rita," he toasted.

Choruses of "Happy Birthday." "Good Luck." "Cheers." Echoed round the garden.

"Now on to the main event, the piñata," said Steve.

He went to put on the blindfold, but Rita stopped him, she looked at him and asked.

"Let me do it Dad, it's my party, can I please?"

"Okay, Rita will break it this time, let's get her ready then," Steve conceded.

The children put the blindfold on Rita and led her underneath the piñata; they spun her round chanting from one to ten as they did, Steve steadied her and passed her the stick. The loud counting from the children roused Gerard from his trance again and he snapped to, he looked over the fence in horror as Rita raised the stick and gave the piñata a two-handed clout, it burst open and the vial of acid shattered on impact, spreading all over Rita, her hair started burning and she was screaming in pain, Steve reached out to move her and got his hands burnt in the process. The acid worked very well, and it was burning large pieces of hair and skin off her cheeks and nose. Luckily Brenda had the wherewithal to spray Rita with the garden hose and drench her completely from head to toe. The children were screaming and crying; some adults were holding them away from the contaminated sweets, which had fallen to the ground. Gerard realized that again something awful had happened and that he had no idea how he got there; in a blind panic just ran away using all his old familiar shortcuts. Back at the house, Steve's hands were burned badly and he couldn't do anything to help, everyone was panicking except Brenda, who as a nurse coped well in situations like these. She plunged Steve's hands into a bucket of cold water to stop the acid burning him more, then called for an ambulance. One thing was for sure the party was totally and utterly ruined, most of the guests were shocked by what they had witnessed, Rita lay prone on the lawn shaking from the ordeal, her hair at the front had been totally dissolved, and her face was red and blistered, her hands were the worst, if it wasn't for the blindfold her eyes would have got it too. A few minutes passed and eventually the ambulance arrived, before Steve was loaded in, he gave an order to Brenda.

"Call Paul, his mobile number is on my phone, only him, nobody else, he will investigate what has happened here, now get Rita and me to the hospital."

Meanwhile, when Gerard didn't show, Emmerich started to panic and when he heard the ambulance coming down the road, drove off in a hurry, not knowing that his trap had taken out the wrong person.

Chapter 14

You'll pay for your actions.

Brenda did what Steve had asked, and went inside to call Paul Collison, she wanted to be with Rita, but one person had to stay and preserve the crime scene, Steve was on his way to hospital with Rita so she composed herself then called the number. Paul took the call, which was easier for Brenda.

"Oh Paul! It's Brenda; There's been an acid attack at Rita's party, she's badly burned on her face and neck and Steve's hands are a mess, before they left in the ambulance, he gave specific instructions to call you personally; to ask you to come over, can you get away?" She asked.

"Yes, I can, they are all over at the mortuary, looking at two more victims, so Simon can man the desk, I'll be right with you," he replied.

Brenda finished the call and went back to the guests, who had remained to support her. The first person to approach her was Brian; he took her to the kitchen and made her some tea.

"There was a man sitting in a Land Rover outside the house, when I brought Rita over, he looked a bit awkward as I passed him and I recognized him, he rented a small car from us yesterday," revealed Brian. Brenda sipped some tea and said.

"Remember to tell Paul when he calls over, what did he look like?"

"He was over sixty, had grey hair, and he spoke with a German accent," said Brian.

"That's a start I suppose, let's hope they hurry up, I want to be at the hospital with Rita," said Brenda, anxiously.

Brian went back out into the garden; he had brought his two young sons David and Calvin to the party, and they were upset and would need a lot of comforting, but first he had to organize the other guests on behalf of the family.

"Everyone who saw anything special that might help the police sort out Rita's attack please stay, and all the other guests, out of respect for Steve, Brenda and Rita, please go home, someone will no doubt be round for a statement and we will call you as soon as we have any news," instructed Brian.

Paul Collison reached his car, before driving off he called Shabby on his mobile. Shabby was in the mortuary with Kenny Purchase, looking at Sean and the headless Phil Barker, who's corpses had just been brought in. He had his phone on silent, when he felt the vibration and he glanced at it and saw it was Paul calling.

"Sorry Guv, but I've got to take this call," he explained. Kenny just rolled his wrist, as if to say carry on and Shabby left the mortuary.

"Paul, how are you? Haven't heard from you in a couple of days, these jokers have kept me occupied," said Shabby, when he answered.

"Jack, Rita Speed has been attacked at her birthday party, Steve got injured as well. They're both at the hospital and he has asked me to investigate, would you be able to assist me please?" Paul asked.

"It will be difficult convincing Kenny, but yes, I would do anything to get out of here, right now," replied Shabby.

Paul set off to Steve's house and Shabby went back to the lab. Kenny had moved over to George Swales body and was looking at him.

"Excuse me, Kenny, I have to leave for an hour or two, if you need me I'll be on the mobile," explained Shabby.

"Wherever you are going, I hope you are quick, we need to crack on with this," said Kenny, a little frustrated.

"Sara is an able assistant she'll take over for now and when I return no more interruptions, I promise," added Shabby.

The swap appealed to Kenny, Sara was very attractive and he had an eye for the ladies, he called Sara through and she wandered in, carrying some samples she had taken off George Swales and put them on top of the counter.

"Can you assist DCI Purchase? Just for an hour or so, I have an errand to take care of personally," instructed Shabby.

Sara dressed in her white gown, and cap then came to the side of Kenny, he looked her up and down and liked what he saw. Shabby winked at the DCI and left the labs. He dressed in his familiar jumpsuit, and drove to Steve's house.

At the hospital, Steve's burns had already been bandaged up; he'd been discharged and allowed to visit Rita. The Consultant came towards him and gave him a face-mask to wear.

"I'm Jill Gaines, I'm looking after your daughter," she said, introducing herself. "The burns on Rita's hands will heal eventually, but she might need a skin graft on her forehead, luckily the blindfold kept it off most of her face, if it weren't for your wife's quick thinking her injuries could have been very severe," she explained.

"I don't think that this was meant for her, the target was me and they missed; well almost," he said, showing her his hands.

"We've got her in an oxygen tent to assist healing and she's quite heavily sedated; we have to keep her like this, until her hands start to heal over, you may go in and be with her, but you can't touch her and she probably won't know you're there, don't worry, this is quite normal our first duty is to the patient and a speedy recovery," explained the Consultant. Steve nodded and went in, he stood and looked; he gulped before sitting down next to her.

"I am sorry Rita, we forgot about you, didn't we? First Jeremy and now you, why did you ask me to move over? If you hadn't then I would be lying there, not you," he said under his breath. He sat looking at her for a while, saying nothing, if Brenda was here, she would be saying all the prayers properly. He then promised himself. "We are going to get the bastards this time sweetheart, whatever it takes. We will bring them down."

Someone coming into the ward broke the silence, it was Helen and Jordanna Stanley, they had come to visit and offer their respects. Steve and Helen hugged each other, feeling the pain of the moment; Jordanna just put a soothing hand on his shoulder.

"I just wanted to come and see Rita, see how you're bearing up," said Helen, sitting down in the chair that Steve had got up from.

Jordanna disappeared to get some drinks, but the Ward Sister told her off for trying to bring drinks into intensive care, she binned them quickly and came back again...

Meanwhile, Paul had reached Steve's place and was walking up the driveway, he rang the bell and Brenda opened the front door. She hugged him,

"Thanks for coming, Paul."

"Show me the scene, and let's see if we can catch this person, shall we?"

Brenda led him to the garden without a word and pointed to the gazebo with the pathetic remains of the piñata still hanging over the pile of gifts, Paul put on some purple gloves and as he walked down to the gazebo, he called back to Brenda.

"I have called Jack and he's coming over, when he calls bring him here please?"

Brenda nodded and waited by the patio. Paul walked around the gazebo, and studied the broken piñata; he didn't want to touch anything until Shabby came, but did note some glass in the debris, then noticed someone approaching.

"Hi, I am Steve's brother Brian, let me know if I can help you with anything," he said.

"Was there anything out of the ordinary before this happened?" Inquired Paul.

"No, it was a normal party, some of the guests who were present when it happened, are waiting for your questions and I've made a list of those guests who have had to go home," explained Brian.

"What about outside, anything strange in the street?" Paul asked.

This made Brian remember what he'd told Brenda.

"It was supposed to be a surprise party, so I fetched Rita from work ostensibly for a dinner party with her folks and as we arrived, I noticed a man sat in his Land Rover, he looked a bit shifty, as if he was trying to hide his face, but I recognized him, he'd hired a car from me the day before."

"What did he look like, can you describe him?" Paul asked.

"He was old, in his sixties, grey hair and green quilted waistcoat, his face was kind looking, but when I passed the Land Rover, he looked uneasy as if he shouldn't have been there; if you want pictures, they will be on the CCTV at my place, Mortal Dean Car Hire on West Road," replied Brian. "I've nearly recalled his name now, its German, something like Dishman, first initial E," revealed Brian, Paul's eyes flickered as he recognized the name. They were interrupted by Shabby's arrival; he walked briskly to the garden and headed straight over to Paul.

"Do you think the target may have been Steve, and Rita was a mistake?" Shabby asked, as he approached.

"Very likely, but right now, I wouldn't rule anything out, I mean who would be nasty enough to put acid into a thing like this?" Paul asked back.

"Let's take it all back to the labs, we'll know more there," assured Shabby.

He bent down and started methodically putting the burst remains of the piñata and its tragic acid-eaten contents into evidence bags including the pieces of glass, for later analysis.

"This will show us what acid we have to deal with," he explained. "And we may get some prints, who knows," he said, putting them in his pocket.

Paul felt deflated that there was nothing of instant importance at the scene and reluctantly put through a call to the station.

"Hi! It's Paul, put me through to Chief Inspector Purchase, please; - - Hello Guv, it's Paul Collison, there's been another attack, - yes, at the Speeds, - acid this time, Steve's arms are burnt but his daughter, Rita, took the main assault on her face, they're both at the hospital; it looks at the moment as if Steve was the intended victim and, best of all, we have a positive Identification on Emmerich Deichmann, sitting in a Land Rover outside the house just before the incident, looking "furtive" according to the witness, so it looks like Steve was right all along; I've talked to most of the guests and no one saw anything interesting, I've got all the names and addresses and I've let them go home, Shabby's already here picking up evidence and we'll see you back at the station."

He went over and told Shabby that he'd informed the boss.

"Good, let's get Mrs Speed to the hospital, I'd imagine she wants to be with Rita," ordered Shabby.

He walked to Brenda and Brian, now standing with her.

"Right we're all finished here, just make the house secure and I'll get you to the hospital, okay?" Suggested Shabby, as he loaded up the bags of evidence and rest of the piñata into his car.

Thanks to all the short cuts, Gerard had been able to get himself from Steve's place to his old home at Brown Gale. He crept cautiously into the farmyard and over to the farmhouse, he rapped on the door and his mother answered, she whooped with delight when she saw it was her son.

"Mother it's been terrible, I need somewhere to crash, you won't believe what's been going on," he said.

She was so pleased to hear him speaking, before he left home, he was so browbeaten and tongue tied, she had hardly heard him talk at all.

"Okay now son, you're here safe, have something to eat and you can explain it all," she soothed, as she ladled out soup and offered him bread, they sat eating in silence, she was just happy Gerard was alive and well.

"The other night, I thought that I dreamt it, when I saw you. But it is really you, why have you waited so long to come back?" Geraldine queried, Gerard greedily finished his food and then he began to explain things.

"I left home because I felt unloved and unwanted. I promised myself that I wouldn't return until Dad was dead, or that I was accepted by the people of this village, one of those has happened, so here I am." Geraldine listened intently and waited for more.

"But it was you that killed Dad, I saw you do it, you saw me afterwards, remember?"

"Just hear me out; when I left, I went to the City and there I met the person who turned my life around, Michaela Deichmann, who not only gave me shelter, she's a Psychiatrist and helped me get through all my troubles. Then I met her Psychology Professor husband, Emmerich, Ah! I see you know the name, Mum, because he found out he's my real father, but you knew that didn't you? I bet you didn't know he was married to the same person who relaxed and re-directed all my traumas? Well I've just found out that he has been manipulating me, under deep hypnosis, to do unspeakable things to all the people who had hurt me, including Dad, just because he didn't like what those people did to me long ago."

Gerard began to cry and she cradled him in her arms, she was deeply shocked to hear all this; Emmerich had always been so kind to her, this was one of the reasons that she fell in love with him.

Detective Chief Inspector Kenny Purchase was in his element, detailing cars and men to go to Emmerich's flat and the university, when Paul arrived in the office.

"Ah! Paul! Young Simon here tells me that we're missing your best witnesses – thirteen blackbirds! Care to tell us all about it?" Paul scowled at Simon, already mentally allocating him all the late shifts for the next month or two, then he mumbled about how unlucky it was and how it might not be all over yet; the reaction from the group was interesting, only Kenny laughed out loud, two smiled, three looked worried and young Pete Wilson crossed himself.

"Okay everyone, comedies over, let's go get this psycho, go through his flat with a fine toothed comb and find that Land Rover."

Simon, still smarting from the way a chance remark had led to both his and Paul's humiliation, was in the lead car that pulled up outside Emmerich's flat, he rang the bell and when the door opened, he got his moment of glory.

"Professor Emmerich Deichmann, I am Simon Hixson of Mortal Dean police, I am arresting you for the assault of Rita Speed. You do not have to say anything. But it may harm your defense if you do not mention when questioned, something which you later rely on in Court. Anything you do say may be taken and given in evidence."

Simon led Emmerich down the steps and bent him into the squad car; knowing he would be bought drinks later at the pub for making the arrest. Lenny Fish, in the other car, radioed the team heading for the university that they had their quarry but to continue and search his office, then he went into the house and started the search, one of the first things he found was a set of car keys on the hall table and a quick search outside revealed the car pool with a Land Rover parked in the bay corresponding to the flat, when he tried the keys, they fitted.

"Right, let's get this to the auto boys for a once over"

Both Kenny and Paul were waiting on the steps of the station when Simon drew up, they walked over to give him congratulations and Emmerich was escorted back to the cells.

"Welcome back Professor! We hope you enjoy the stay this time, we've kept your usual room open for you," mocked Paul, pretending to be a hotel manager. Emmerich raised his head and confidently replied.

"I will be out of here in two hours, once my lawyer arrives."

"Oh! Then we'll make your stay here more comfortable for you, shall we! Leave the cuffs on men," ordered Paul, so they took him to the cells still in handcuffs.

"Well done, the drinks are on me later," said Paul, pleased with his men, he still had the fifty pounds in his pocket that Steve had given him for that stupid bet that seemed an age ago, this would be the ideal occasion to spend it.

Shabby arrived with Brenda at the hospital and they quickly found Steve. He was drinking coffee outside of Rita's ward. Brenda kissed him and went in to see their daughter; she put her hands to her mouth when she saw Rita lying still and fast asleep. Her face covered over with light dressing to prevent infection. Helen gave Brenda comfort as she began to cry, and they stood hugging each other. Jordanna walked out to give them space, and watched from outside the door. Shabby was talking to Steve and he explained a couple of details found at the scene.

"I'm very pleased to see you walking around so soon, you think that Rita was the wrong victim, am I correct?" He asked.

"It was a one off, usually I, as head of the household, would break the damned thing and the kids take the sweets, but she insisted on doing it, this is just what I didn't want," said Steve.

"The good thing is she is still alive and should recover from this, others aren't so lucky, if it is the same person we're after, then this showed leniency," said Shabby, with his usual logic.

Steve nodded and accepted he was lucky, but he was still feeling angry about it.

"Did you find anything at the scene?" Inquired Steve.

"Some pieces of glass, these will be taken for analysis, but your brother identified maybe Prof Deichmann, lurking outside in a Land Rover, just before it happened; there's coppers all over the place looking for him," revealed Shabby. "Anyway, I must get back before Kenny blows a gasket."

Just then Helen came out of the ward, to give Brenda some privacy with Rita, she drank her cold coffee and studied Steve, he caught her looking.

"What is it?" He quizzed.

"I have something to tell you, about yesterday, Jordanna brought that Gerry person back to our house in the morning, I think it is the man you are looking for," she confessed.

"Gerard Swales? That's his name, he was here in our street and you didn't fucking tell anyone?" Steve bellowed at her, all the people stopped and stared.

"He ran off, but I am sure it was him, Paul showed me the photo, I screamed but nobody heard me," she admitted.

"If you had told somebody yesterday, Rita wouldn't be lying there, now look at her, I can't believe you didn't say anything, look what he's fucking done to us!"

Helen stood firm and shouted back.

"You said he killed my Jeremy and I was protecting Jordanna, what were you doing? Jeremy and Rita loved each other; now look at them. You should have protected her more." Steve looked down, suddenly going very quiet, as if this was a catalyst.

"I'm going after him and I will take him down."

He was seething and left the hospital to find Gerard, he would be the one to bring him in. Helen went back to Brenda to tell her what just happened.

Brenda just said.

"If Steve has something to deal with and he's gone into his 'quiet mode' it is just better to let him get on with it, he'll come back."

At that moment, Rita's fingers twitched as she began to rouse from her sedation. Brenda pressed the alarm and the staff nurse came rushing in.

"No, not just yet, we'd rather give her skin more recovery time before we can wake her, Nurse!"

After a fresh sedative injection, Rita drifted back to sleep, Brenda sat back down and waited for the moment when she could speak to her again and offered up prayers. Jordanna had witnessed the argument between her mother and Steve, she had heard Gerard's name mentioned. She went outside and texted a warning to Gerard that Steve was coming for him and that she still loved him. She added a photo of herself wearing see through underwear to cheer him up and keep him keen. She went back up to kiss her mother goodbye then left the hospital determined to find Gerard before Steve.

Back at Brown Gale, Gerard had taken a shower and cleaned himself up, downstairs he could hear Georgina and Gregg talking, his heart in his mouth, he hadn't seen them since he left, he slowly walked downstairs to speak to them. They were in the sitting room discussing the business, as soon as Gerard walked in Gregg got up and punched him on the jaw, knocking him back through the door; Gerard had expected a bit of coolness, maybe hostility, but not this, then he was astonished when Georgina got in the way to protect him.

"Stop this, it isn't necessary, we're adults not thugs," she shouted.

"He killed Dad!" Gregg yelled and sat down again with his head on his arms, "I know he was a useless drunk, but I loved him, he was my Dad and he killed him." He started to snivel.

"Well I'm glad he did, do you know why? When Gerry left, Dad turned his abuse on me, not smacking, but touching me and making me do things girls shouldn't do with their fathers," she revealed.

Gregg stopped and helped Gerard up; he never knew this until now. Geraldine had also heard it all from the hallway and entered the lounge.

"My poor darling, I never knew, why didn't you say anything? Well! He isn't going to do that again, now is he?"

Geraldine hugged her daughter and Gregg made his apologies to Gerard. They all went through to the kitchen and began to catch up on all the news. All of Gerard's stories came out and his siblings just listened to it, they didn't know anything about the bullying at school or his real father, but Geraldine explained all that and it now dawned on them why Gerard was so different to them. Then Gerard changed the tone.

"Listen I'm pretty sure that I've done something bad today, I came out of a trance at the Speed's house, you know the Detective? People were being hurt and somehow I'm sure I'm responsible. I must turn myself in."

At that moment, his mobile signaled a message. He read what Jordanna wrote and gazed at her picture; knowing that she loved him, gave him inner strength. He went into the yard and waited, as if knowing by instinct that someone was coming for him and now was the time to clear the sheet.

Steve left the hospital and went straight home, swapped his clothes for clean ones, then took a quick drink of brandy to steady his nerve, not knowing what to expect from Gerard when he met him. The most likely place for Gerard would be, at the Swales' farm, Mrs Swales reactions when her husband had been killed were all wrong. He remembered the route to the farm, and was there in less than ten minutes. His car rolled to a stop and he stepped out, there stood the person responsible for Rita's agony, all his hurt boiled up and he ran over to where Gerard was waiting, he punched him twice in the mouth and Gerard fell over, Steve gave him another thump in the ribs, which made Gerard groan, having been hit there three nights before.

"Stop hitting him, he's gentle, don't hurt him, please!" Geraldine shrieked, as she came out, Steve gave him one more punch for good measure, leaving Gerard out of breath.

"He's going to hand himself in, he knows your daughter got hurt and thinks he's responsible," said Georgina, who was now between Steve and her brother. Steve backed off and allowed Gerard up, his sister held him steady.

"I will go with you, but you must bring in Emmerich Deichmann, he's the person behind it all," explained Gerard and then looked at his mother.

"Mum, I'm sorry, I should have spoken to you sooner, Gregg and Georgie will take care of you and I'll speak to you soon as everything's sorted," said Gerard, then got in the car with Steve, and they drove to the police station.

"Oh, by the way, we've already got Professor Deichmann in custody, he's probably singing about you now. Seems like the type, to let you take it all," revealed Steve.

Gerard knew about the case in the Land Rover so felt he had the upper hand. Steve drove to the police station. When Steve arrived with Gerard, the whole place fell quiet; he slowly walked Gerard to the booking desk, and said.

"Book this man in for the murder of eleven Mortal Dean citizens, will you Paul? By the book, official caution the lot."

The station erupted with spontaneous applause for this unexpected event, with Kenny still at the mortuary; this would leave a sour taste in his mouth. Paul took Gerard away, completed the formalities, then took him down to the cells, pushed him in and locked the door.

Jordanna arrived back in Mortal Dean, she now knew Gerard's surname and the Swales' lived at Brown Gale farm, so she started to walk there not knowing that Gerard was already in custody. Whilst she walked, she tried Gerard's mobile that was still on the kitchen table. Geraldine noticed the vibrating phone and picked it up, she saw it was Jordanna and pressed answer.

"Gerry, is that you, look Steve Speed knows about you and he is on his way to bring you in, you should get away, I'll help you, so I am coming over," she said.

"Sorry, my dear, I'm Geraldine, his mother and I am afraid he has already handed himself over to the police," she revealed.

"Oh! Shit! Look I'm half way to you, is it all right if I come by? Let's see if we can do something to help him, shall we?" She asked.

"If you genuinely want to help, come on over, I'll be waiting for you," Geraldine replied.

The conversation ended and Jordanna began to think of ways to aid Gerard, could she spring him from the police? Geraldine had been told all about Jordanna and Gerard's feelings towards her, and as she came down the lane Geraldine went to meet her, they embraced as if they were two close friends and began to hatch a plan.

Chapter 15

Mystery murder tour.

The cell door opened; Emmerich could see his Lawyer, Basil Granger, standing beside Paul who asked him to stand up before taking off his handcuffs.

"You have ten minutes with your man here, then we're taking you up for questioning," instructed Paul.

Emmerich, still unaware of Gerard's arrest, had a confident air about his chances of going free.

"Emmerich, whatever scrape you've got yourself into, I don't think I can help, unless you give me everything you know," said Basil. Emmerich stared at him and then started to speak.

"They have arrested me for an assault of a girl, I've never met, they haven't told me who she is and how she was hurt. The only thing they have is that I was outside the house when it happened," he said, feeling sure of his cover story.

"Right give me every little detail, and we'll work from there, if it's as you say, you'll be free in an hour, I give you my word," promised Basil. Emmerich gave his version of why he was there in Mortal Dean, the circumstances of being outside Steve's house at the time of the incident and his previous questioning by the police. Prepared with this information, Basil was ready for Paul to take Emmerich for questioning. Paul opened the door of Emmerich's cell, took Emmerich by the arm and walked him to interview room two. Paul sat Emmerich in a chair and then left the room. Basil made himself comfortable and they waited. Darren and Lana entered the interview room and closed the door behind them. Darren took out some cassettes, laid them on the table and sat down. Lana put one of the tapes into the recorder, pressed the record button and the questioning began.

"In the interview room are myself, Detective Inspector Darren Lane, Detective Sergeant Lana Scannell, Professor Emmerich Deichmann, and Mr Basil Granger, counsel for the Accused," said Darren. "The time is eighteen fifteen and the date is the 29th of August." Darren then looked across to Emmerich. "Please tell us why you were outside the house of Detective Speed at fifteen thirty this afternoon, Professor?" Came his opening question.

"You do not have to answer any questions Emmerich, just answer 'no comment'," instructed Basil.

"Nonsense Basil, I can explain, you see, I had remembered some information which I forgot about when he last questioned me. I went to his house and wanted to speak with him, but when I got there and noticed a party was taking place, I decided to wait for it to finish," he replied.

"What we think is, you were questioned earlier and we were a little too close to the truth and you decided to stop Detective Steve Speed from making further inquiries, is that about the measure of it, Professor?" Probed Lana.

"No, it is as I have said, just because I was there, that does not mean that I want to give harm," Emmerich answered coolly, although he knew that Lana was spot on. Emmerich was lying and Basil smiled to himself; because he knew his client was handling the situation well; his work would be easy, just sit there and listen.

While Darren and Lana were questioning Emmerich, Steve and Paul were preparing to question Gerard, Paul opened the cell door, Gerard was sitting quiet and still, nothing about him stood out, his character and posture was not one of a crazy serial killer. Gerard looked at Paul, waiting for him to speak.

"You must come with us now, we need to get to the bottom of this," said Paul and led him to the interview room. Steve was waiting when he arrived and with him was the station medical examiner; Steve ushered Gerard into the room and after sitting him down, asked.

"Before we begin, would you mind if we take some DNA and fingerprint samples from you?"

Gerard just shrugged, and the medic proceeded to collect DNA from his cheek, then fingerprints.

"Right sit down then Mr Swales, we have a whole lot of questions to ask, and you need to do some explaining," he clicked on the tape machine. "The time is eighteen fifteen and the date is the 29th of August, present are Detective Constable Steve Speed, Sergeant Paul Collison, together with Gerard Swales, who is being questioned about the frequency of unexplained deaths in and around Mortal Dean."

"Let's start with an easy question then, why did you hurt Rita Speed?" Paul asked.

"I didn't know why and I don't know how; I just sort of came to, looking over the fence and realizing that something was very wrong, just like at the reservoir," answered Gerard. "I don't remember how I got there, I just know what I saw."

"How could you not know how you got there?" Steve asked, a little confused.

"I can't explain it, whatever happens to me is a mystery, and my memory is affected somehow. I just have the facts and that is all," answered Gerard.

"Why did you say that Emmerich was in on it, please explain?" Paul asked, a bit savvier in his questioning.

"I think he was the one who drove me there, he has been controlling me somehow by hypnosis," Gerard revealed. Paul stopped the tape and stood up.

"That's the biggest load of old bollocks that I've ever heard, but to give you the benefit of the doubt and to let you hang yourself even more. I'll go next door to check this out, while I am gone, please relax and see if you can think of any other wonderful stories that can help us?" He said before leaving Steve with Gerard.

"I just want to know what turns you into a killer and while we're here I will find it," Steve promised.

Gerard just sat waiting for Paul to return, he had already felt how much Steve hated him, and didn't want to stir things up.

"How did you get those cuts on your face, hey? Surely, you'd remember getting those, I would," noted Steve. "The minute I work out what makes you tick, everyone will see your true colors, you can't fool us with this shy Mr Nice Guy routine forever."

Meanwhile, next door, Paul knocked and put his head round the door.

"Sorry to interrupt, but something has come to our attention, can I speak to you a second?" He asked; Darren and Lana stepped out of the room.

"We have Mr Swales next door and he says that Emmerich brought him to Steve's place," revealed Paul.

"Well he's saying he was on his own and he wasn't involved at all, but we'll put it to him, thanks Paul," replied Darren, and Lana smiled and they both went back in to continue.

"You say you were alone in the area when this attack took place but we have a witness who saw you driving there, swears you had a passenger," said Lana.

"I feel your witness is unreliable, I was driving alone," replied Emmerich.

"Well actually my witness seems very reliable, his name is Gerard Swales and he was sitting alongside you at the time, wasn't he Professor?" She added. Emmerich was completely floored by her sucker punch, and didn't even answer.

"My client can't answer that question, as it may incriminate him in other activities, made by this Gerard Swales," Basil chipped in.

"He doesn't have to answer, we knew Mr Swales was with him, he says so, and that is good enough for us" said Darren.

Knowing Gerard was in custody made Emmerich realize that he would have to be more evasive with his answers.

"So, as we were about to ask you, is there anything you want to contribute? Why were you outside Steve's house, if you don't tell us, we'll charge you with aiding and abetting, at the very least, because I feel that you're in this right up to your perfectly knotted tie," said Lana.

"It is down to you to prove my guilt, I don't have to say anything," said Emmerich cleverly.

"All you can charge my client with is loitering, until you can come up with any evidence to the contrary, then you must release him," added Basil.

"I am sorry but we don't intend to release him just yet, the lowest charge he'll be facing is attempted murder. You may have an hour with your Brief, Professor, and we will resume then. Interview terminated at

Twenty hundred hours." Darren turned off the tape; they left the room and guided Emmerich back to his cell. Basil went in with him and they began to urgently plan strategy. Darren and Lana went for refreshments and Lana rang her boss at the labs. Kenny wanted reports and had to be kept informed.

Paul returned to Gerard

"Can you tell us about your hunting holiday, with the Professor, Mr Swales?" Quizzed Steve.

"He wanted company when he went hunting and asked if I'd like to join him, he brought Saul along briefly, don't ask me why," answered Gerard.

"What happened to the weapons you were using?" Asked Paul.

"I believe that they were stolen, the window got broken," Gerard said, remembering his father's call.

"Well we can tell you what happened to these weapons, they're at the Forensics lab, after you left them behind with Major Richard Joiner's body," revealed Steve, noticing Gerard shift uneasily on hearing the name.

"Ah! So, you know who he is? Well I know a little story about you Gerard. When you were a boy, he used to pick on you didn't he and so did his friends, is this what made you go out and kill them?" Asked Steve.

"No, I have control of my feelings about them and bear them no animosity, Richard was just insecure about his popularity and used his friends to hide it," said Gerard defensively.

Steve tried another option.

"How do you know Jordanna Stanley? She's a fine girl, did you know she was Jeremy's sister and Richard's cousin?"

"I'm sorry, I didn't know that, she's just a girl that I met at my gym that I go to, she wasn't anything like her bully of a brother," Gerard answered coolly.

Steve suddenly snapped, stood up and pulled Gerard by the shirt.

"Where are you? There's a killer in there somewhere, show me him?" He shouted, shaking him. Paul had to intervene.

"Steve stop that please, give the guy a break, you can't force a confession, let it come naturally," he soothed. Steve released Gerard and stormed out of the room, Paul stood and turned off the tape.

"You can have a break, and we will resume this later. Come on I'll take you back to your cell," said Paul.

Gerard stood and Paul led him by the arm to his cell. The cell door was slammed shut behind him. Gerard was biding his time; he wanted Emmerich deep up to his neck, before confessing anything.

The two samples of DNA from Emmerich and Gerard were ready and Kenny had gone to collect them to hurry things along, whilst Shabby was waiting for the results his mobile buzzed in his pocket, he made his excuses to Sara and took the call, as he answered his heart gave a little jump as he heard Georgina's tantalizing voice.

"Mr Stores, I needed to call you, they have my brother in custody. I felt that I should speak to you about things that happened to us, because of our Daddy, when we were younger."

"Okay, then as soon as I've finished here, we can meet, where are you now?" Shabby asked.

"I am outside Mortal Dean police station, so if you can be quick, then I would appreciate it," answered Georgina, her soft words affecting him, he realized how much he wanted to see her again.

"Remain where you are? I will be quick as possible," he answered, as he returned to Sara's side and she revealed the results of the acid used.

"Definitely, sulphuric' acid, easily stored, and the most effective acid to cause injury," she said.

Just then Kenny returned to them with the DNA results, he handed them to Shabby who studied them, then said.

"The DNA taken from the two suspects are such of a similar pattern, I can only deduce, Emmerich and Gerard are biologically father and son," he revealed, just then the phone rang. Kenny picked it up.

"Kenny Purchase."

"Good evening, Guv, Auto Labs here, we've looked over your Land Rover, subject to final analysis, we have soil samples from the tyres linking this vehicle to both the reservoir and Brown Gale farm and as a bonus, hidden under a coat in the back, we've found an overnight case containing one of those German anti-contamination coats, you know, a sort of rubberized overcoat with a hood and it's covered in blood stains, plus other bits and pieces. It's all on its way over, when Shabby gets his hands on this lot, he'll think it's Christmas already."

"Right let's get all this to the team at the station, they'll need this to fill in the gaps, with this little lot we'll send both these jokers down for good," crowed Kenny. "Sara, can you finish up here, whilst we do this, you've been very helpful, thank you," Sara continued as normal, tidying things up without a word.

Back at the station, unaware of the forensic breakthrough, Steve and Paul were getting ready for another round with Gerard; Steve took all the photos off the incident board.

"Let's take these? If his memory is shaky these may help him remember."

"Okay, but take it slow don't just rush in with them. Take your time or he'll just clam up again," warned Paul.

Steve slipped the pictures into a file so that nobody could see; then they fetched Gerard to the interview room. Paul closed the door and Steve started the tape again.

"Welcome back Mr Swales, I hope you've had time to reflect?" Asked Paul. Gerard just nodded.

"When we broke off half an hour ago, you were saying that you don't remember hurting Rita, is that still correct?" Steve started the questions.

"That's right, I just sort of came to and saw it happen and I am sorry for that," replied Gerard.

"Okay, we believe you're sorry about Rita, but what about him and him?" Steve asked, as he revealed the pictures of Sean and the headless Phil. Gerard shifted a little uneasily on seeing the photos.

"No, I don't feel sorry for them, they tried to rape Jordanna," Gerard snapped. "They deserved to die,"

Yes! Finally, some emotion, thought Steve.

"Nobody deserves to die, Mr Swales, that is an unfair statement, would you like to tell us all about it?" Paul said, feeling a bit angry.

"Again, I just woke up at the reservoir, the water was flooding in, all red, I can't remember getting there, just waking to see them dying, I tried to save them but the water was too deep," said Gerard.

"Woke up? Like you were in a trance or something?" Asked Paul.

Gerard nodded and Steve brought out another photograph, this was of George Swales.

"Why did you kill your own father, Mr Swales? Did he deserve to die too?" Steve asked, with a scornful tone. Gerard's agitation began to boil over, and he answered.

"That man is not my father, he is a bully, a drunk and a coward, he was jealous of my Mum and me, because she loved me more than him, but I have no memory of killing him."

Paul had noted the change in Gerard's behaviour while they were asking questions.

"Okay, we'll rest easy there a moment, I'll get us some refreshments," said Paul, turning off the recorder.

Steve nodded and Gerard just sat looking straight back at Steve, not even hearing Paul say this. Paul got up and left leaving Steve and Gerard alone. Steve stood and pushed the door to, then picked up the file again, he held it open, then started bringing out pictures one by one, so that Gerard could see.

"See these people? They are all dead because of you, look at them, Zach, Stuart, Colin, Luke, Jez, Richard, Betty and Caitlin. Don't you feel anything for them? I know about your injury Swales, can't be easy wandering around looking like that, knowing that the women will be scared away," mocked Steve.

Gerard's eyes began to glaze over, as if something possessed him. Steve began jabbing at the pictures, yelling.

"You bastard, you've killed these people, I'm going to count down from ten, and I want some answers. Ten, nine, eight, seven, six, five, four, three, two, one!"

Gerard's trance was upon him, he seemed to double in strength, he lunged at Steve, grabbed him whilst twisting him round with his arm up his back. He had his hand under Steve's chin and held him tightly; Steve tried struggling, to no avail, Gerard was too strong,

"This is what you wanted isn't it? To see me like this, do you think you can do anything while I'm this way?" Asked Gerard. Steve knew that Gerard could kill him, and he had to co-operate. At that moment Paul returned with the teas, he looked in disbelief at what he was confronted with.

"How did this go all tits up Steve?" Paul asked, and then saw all the pictures on the table, he realized that's how, just what he warned him about.

"Don't make any silly moves, or I'll break his fucking neck," threatened Gerard, as Paul backed away, Steve felt the pressure under his neck and knew Gerard wasn't joking.

"If you want to know why these people were killed, I will show you," explained Gerard and shunted Steve out of the room.

"Give me your handcuffs and put them on him?" Ordered Gerard, still holding Steve tightly.

Paul did what he was told and Gerard moved with Steve out of the custody suite, down the corridor to the exit and out into the car park, just as Shabby and Kenny came driving into the car park. They saw Gerard had Steve and if he wanted to could break his neck easily.

Georgina was still waiting and came over to Gerard, she tried to stop him, but he just shoved her to one side, snatched her scarf and tied it around Steve's eyes. He searched Steve's pockets and found his keys, then pushed him over to his Mercedes and bundled him into the back. He got in the front, and sped away from the station. Kenny was fuming, because they had let Gerard go, whilst his fellow officers feared for Steve, they knew how devastating Gerard could be in this mood. Gerard raced away to the scene of his first killing. He screeched to a halt outside the remains of the barn, grabbed Steve out from the back and walked him over to the ruins. He took off the blindfold and Steve saw where he was.

"Why have you brought me here?" Steve asked, Gerard pointed then spoke as if reciting from a script.

"This is where Betty and Caitlin trapped me and hung me up, you mentioned my injuries, well this is where it took place, now you can see the relevance of their punishment, can't you?" Said Gerard requiring a response.

"But they didn't kill you, did they though? Who was it that cut you down?" Replied Steve, trying to calm him down.

Gerard just pulled Steve away, put the blindfold back on and shoved him into the car and drove away again. The drive took a while but eventually they stopped, Gerard got out and again slid Steve out from the back. Steve felt himself being marched down a muddy lane, they stopped and off came the blindfold and he saw that he was at the paintball centre.

"The hut has been taken to the lab, sorry about that mate. I suppose you're going to give me some spiel on how Richard deserved his death?" Steve said, trying harder to break Gerard's rage.

"Richard Joiner gave me very little respect, when we were children, he and his mates hurt me every chance they got, I can still see him grinning at me, he was a merciless arsehole, we enjoyed setting that trap," revealed Gerard.

"He saved his comrades, when they were bombed, he'd come home for his best friend's memorials, and you slaughtered him like it didn't matter," revealed Steve.

This still didn't budge Gerard, it was like talking to a zombie; he just whisked Steve away to his next kill zone, Luke's house. Gerard stopped again and sat for a few moments, then, instead of getting out, he sat Steve up and pulled down the blindfold.

"This is Luke's place, he was the worst of the lot, always down on me from the beginning, if it wasn't Dad at home, it was Luke at school, he kept picking and picking, he just had to go," said Gerard. "When my father told me that he was a builder it was planned to bury him in concrete," he added.

Steve noticed the extra person being included in the terrifying narrative. Gerard just floored the accelerator and drove to the scene of Jez's accident. When he stopped, Steve looked out and could see from the other side of the field, four squad cars coming their way. He decided to try and keep him talking until they got to him.

"This is where Jez met his end, I still enjoy the look of terror in his eyes as I swung the lorry into him," revealed Gerard.

"I have already seen these places, after you'd been there, nothing but devastation, Gerard, all you are doing is reminding me of that, so please can we go back and we can tie up this case, what do you say?" Pleaded Steve.

Gerard shrugged and drove away, Steve hoped that his colleagues had worked out by now that Gerard was revisiting the scenes of his crimes and they would be there waiting for him. It was a long chase to the chicken factory, over the other side of the village, two of the squad cars had caught up with Gerard, they were right on his tail, Steve knew that there were four altogether. The other two must have driven round the other way to trap him. Sure enough, round the next bend, there they were, half blocking the road, Gerard drove straight for the slight gap and Steve winced as his beloved Mercedes smashed into them, making the first squad car spin around, clouting the second one and completely blocking the road. Gerard continued to race away towards the chicken factory.

Chapter 16

Scot-free.

Whilst the police were chasing around trying to catch up with Gerard and his hostage, Geraldine and Jordanna were at Brown Gale Farm, talking about Gerard and what happened to him as a child. Geraldine told her about the kids who bullied him and about his father's violence towards them both. Jordanna felt bad that her own brother was involved but she just felt even more love for Gerard for how he managed to get over it all. Geraldine also told her what Emmerich had done to Gerard, conditioning him to do all those attacks.

"I knew he wouldn't have done all those things if he was normal, Emmerich must be some kind of evil genius to have covered it up so well," said Jordanna, Geraldine nodded and then continued.

"This is why he is with the police, he said that he 'came to' at the Speed's place and witnessed the terror and pain of the acid attack with only a vague feeling that he was involved somehow and also that Emmerich took him to do it, when he realized what had happened, he came here first and then handed himself in."

"My goodness that was a brave thing to do, we need to explain to the police that they've got it all wrong," replied Jordanna, at that moment the kitchen telephone rang and Geraldine rose to answer it.

"Mother, it's Georgie, Gerard has escaped. He's kidnapped Steve Speed and driven off with him." She revealed; sounding a little panicked.

"How is he, does he seem okay?" Her mother asked.

"He's changed, he's acting crazily, the police are worried that he might kill the man he's taken," Georgina replied.

"Right okay, you stay there and we will try and find him, any idea where he might be heading?" Geraldine asked.

"The police said he was heading north, that could mean the Poultry Factory," replied Georgina.

"Right, Gregg is just getting the wagon ready for his run at ten, I will send Jordanna with him and they will try to get to him first," she explained.

Meanwhile back at the station, Lana Scannell brought a prisoner up to the desk,

"Hey, Boss! Look what I just brought in? It's Saul Reading,"

"I know that name, he was part of that hunting party, now we're really getting somewhere." Said Kenny, delightedly.

"Not only that, Guv, that's also the name of the person who hired the cement lorry."

"That's too much of a coincidence, get him into the interview room and grill him like toast."

Saul was led into a room, told to sit down, Lana and Darren took their seats,

"Right, Mr Reading, you've been read your rights, now you're going to tell us all you know or you'll be facing up to eight years for aiding and abetting eleven murders," Saul started to explain.

"Okay, Okay. I'll tell you everything, but first I want to bargain for leniency, I only helped the Professor, I didn't actually do anything, he just wanted tools and stuff."

Lana left Darren with Saul and quickly informed Kenny, who immediately agreed to the proposition, she returned to the interview room.

"Alright, Mr Reading, Chief Inspector Purchase, who is leading this investigation, has agreed to look favorably upon any involvement by yourself if you co-operate fully during the rest of this investigation. Right, first, what's your connection to Professor Deichmann."

"I'm a badly paid lab assistant at the university, to supplement my wages, I grow marijuana in a disused basement under the labs nothing big, just a couple of dozen plants, enough to supply a few snotty students, well, the Professor found out and since then has made me his personal slave. I am also a part time driver at FastKrete, again for extra cash; anyway, last week he asks me to take a load of concrete to the Mortal Dean Crossroads, get out of the lorry and catch a bus home, well you can imagine my feelings when I hear on the news that a cement lorry has been involved in a hit and run fatality. Next, he orders me to bring some provisions out to his hunting cabin, I spent some of the evening with him and his son, he's a nice enough lad, next Emmerich tells me to leave, I asked about the weapons and he was acting strangely, the Prof then says if anyone asks about this, I was there for the week. But the thing that really freaked me out and why I pissed off to Yorkshire was that he wanted my assistance in filling vials with sulphuric acid as a booby trap for someone. Listen, I might have bent the law a little, but that nutter needs to be locked up. So, if you keep your side of the bargain and go easy with me over the grass, then I'm prepared to stand up in court and swear." Lana left the interview room, went to Kenny's office and gave him a quick outline of Saul's evidence; Kenny, who knew exactly when a case turned in his favour, said:

"We've got most of the details, nobody let the Professor know that Gerard has escaped, he must believe that he is still here, turning the screw on his old man."

Lana agreed and returned with Darren ready to question the Professor again. Simon brought Emmerich back to the interview room with Basil hurrying behind him. Emmerich was sat down again and Lana sat opposite him, he noticed that she was holding something different this time but didn't feel too nervous. Darren and Kenny stepped into the room and Simon closed the door.

"Right I hope you enjoyed your hour to think over your position? Let's get back to business," said Darren. "When you left us you said we should prove your guilt, instead of accusing you of doing something, well we have found shed loads to substantiate our inquiries," revealed Lana.

"What is it, Inspector? Remember I never entered the party," replied Emmerich. Basil smiled at Lana in a smug way, then Kenny stepped in – he always liked to be in at the kill

"Professor, I'm Chief Inspector Purchase of the Serious Crimes Squad, it's no longer just about poor Rita, you are now being formally charged with instigating, assisting and abetting the murders of Sean Curle, Phillip Barker, Zach Dagan, Stuart Warner, Colin Rusdale, Luke Jarvis, Jeremy Stanley, Richard Joiner, Betty and Caitlin Jones. Your Land Rover can be placed at two of the murder sites and your contamination coat, complete with bloodstains has been found in the back; your 'friend' Saul Reading is in custody, singing like a canary about glass vials, cement lorries and other stuff. Do you have anything else to say? - - - - I thought not! Nick him!"

Emmerich just slumped in his chair, all the bravado was gone, dismissed Basil with a wave of his hand and allowed himself to be led back to the cells.

In the corridor of the police station, Georgina approached Shabby and tugged his jacket.

"I would like to speak with you a moment, if you can spare me some time?" She asked.

Shabby couldn't deny his strong attraction towards Georgina; he'd never felt this way before.

"Oh! Hi! Georgina, it would be a pleasure to sit and listen to you speak, let's find a comfortable room," he led her to an empty office with blinds around the windows and ushered her in, she stood until Shabby sat down and then she did the same.

"What seems to be the trouble? You spoke about your brother on the telephone, what is this family history that you mentioned?" He asked.

"Yes, I think that you ought to know that when Gerard was a small boy, my Dad was so bad to him, he beat him with his belt and even used a cattle prod on him, he was bed-wetting and Dad hated it but the more he punished him, the worse it got," she revealed.

"George punished him for bed-wetting is that all?" Shabby quizzed.

"Well, Father was an alcoholic, he never believed that Gerard was his son and recently Gerard accidentally found out that it was true all along," she replied.

"Yes, we know that Emmerich is his real father, the DNA samples match conclusively," explained Shabby.

"Gerard was also bullied and beaten up at school all the time; finally, he couldn't take it anymore, when he left school, he also left home. We found his clothes by an estuary, we never found his body and thought he was dead," she added.

"I can see now why he had a reason to kill George, and the others, being tormented this way," soothed Shabby.

"Well, the abuse didn't end there, when Gerard disappeared, Daddy turned to me, I was thirteen and 'blossoming' he would say, he made me do things with him which I hated, he was so strong and continued until I was nearly eighteen when I plucked up the courage to say no, it cost me a split lip and a black eye, but at least it stopped," she began to sob and Shabby held her tightly, absorbing her anger and her pain

Back over at the north end of Mortal Dean, Gerard had completed his drive to the chicken factory, and bundled Steve out of his car, he pulled him by the handcuffs behind him. There weren't any police cars yet; Steve couldn't even hear any sirens. It was approaching ten o'clock and the shift was about to change, any minute people would swamp the car park getting to their cars to go home. This allowed Gerard some cover and pulled Steve through the crowd as the hooter sounded and it got busy very quickly, nobody took any notice of Steve and Gerard; they just wanted to get home. Gerard followed the crowd filing into the factory, once inside he pulled Steve down the corridor to the plant room, shoved Steve in and closed the door behind him.

"This is where Colin met his end, he was such a dickhead, bullied everyone at school who was smaller than himself. He got the cold steel from me, right across his throat, just what he deserved," said Gerard.

"There's that word again 'deserved', you can't justify a death like that, just because somebody didn't like you at school, there is nothing self-righteous about it," replied Steve, waiting for a moment when he could get away. "Anyway, what about the other two, you cut them down in cold blood, how can you justify their deaths? You weren't thinking straight were you Gerard, just like now, you're not in the right frame of mind, are you?" Steve was probing away, trying to break Gerard's trance.

"They were part of the eight people who shot me with paint pellets, if they hadn't followed Colin here, they would still be alive, no witnesses," Gerard replied.

"So, you got bit of paint on you! Big deal, something tells me you were put up to this, does somebody else know about your story? Perhaps they were the ones who were pissed off and then had you do their dirty work for them," reasoned Steve, searching for the connection to Emmerich.

By this time the police had arrived at the factory, they had phoned the owners of the place and had them clear everyone out of the building. The factory was deserted, accept for Steve and Gerard, on the other side of the compound Gregg pulled his wagon to the loading doors, waiting for his cargo of chickens to be unloaded, Jordanna, who was with him, jumped down from the cab and ran through the factory searching for Gerard, the place was massive so she had to spend a lot of time looking in the wrong places, she didn't call out, because she knew that Steve would be with him and she remained quiet as she could. Gregg began to unload the chickens himself, when nobody turned up to help. Back round the front of the factory, Paul had organized his officers, blocking all the exits and then with his loud haler began demanding that Gerard release his colleague.

"GERARD! WE KNOW YOU ARE IN THERE, LOOK YOU ARE IN BIG TROUBLE ALREADY, JUST GIVE YOURSELF UP, YOU DON'T REALLY WANT TO HURT ANYBODY," coaxed Paul.

Jordanna heard this and headed towards it, hoping it would sound again. Back inside the plant room Gerard had held Steve to him after hearing the sirens; he put his hand back under Steve's chin, reinforcing his threat.

"Look Gerard, stop this now and we can all get out of this alive, what do you say?" Steve pleaded, but Gerard increased his hold.

"They don't know where we are yet, I see no need to give you up, not at the moment," said Gerard coldly.

"Look, that's Paul on the loud haler, he does know where we are, you haven't much time left, so come on release the choke-hold?" He pleaded again.

"I AM GOING TO COUNT TO TEN, AND IF YOU DON'T COME OUT, MY COLLEAGUES ARE COMING IN FOR YOU," shouted Paul again and then began counting.

Jordanna had reached the plant room but couldn't hear anything; she waited for the counting to begin and stood quietly.

"ONE, TWO, THREE, FOUR, FIVE, SIX, SEVEN, EIGHT, NINE, TEN, RIGHT WE ARE COMING IN," Paul's voice echoed through the empty factory.

As Paul finished counting Gerard snapped out of his trance, he released Steve straight away and in horror noticed where he was. "Why are we here? How did we get here and why are you in handcuffs?

"What, you don't remember all this?" Countered Steve, who had got up, instead of attacking Gerard, realized that somebody else made Gerard like this.

"I don't remember getting from the station to here, how did it happen?" Gerard asked softly.

"I showed you some photographs, and you kind of flipped out back there, you've been out and about, now we've ended up in here," explained Steve, Gerard unlocked the door and they both walked out of the plant room to find Jordanna standing outside.

"Listen Gerard didn't mean to hurt those people, Emmerich had hypnotized him and forced him to kill on his behalf," she explained. Steve looked from Jordanna to Gerard and he nodded back.

"It's true, he is my real father, when he found out about all those tortures, he made me go and kill them, and then reconditioned me to forget about it, if you want any confirmation speak to his wife, Michaela Deichmann, the psychiatrist," he explained.

Steve just shrugged. "Listen, I have to stop Paul moving in, but I need my mobile, it's in my jacket pocket and I can't reach," said Steve. Jordanna instantly got the phone out. Steve found Paul's number and called it.

"Steve is everything alright? Has he hurt you?" Paul asked, when he answered.

"No, I'm fine, completely unharmed and I've broken the case wide open, Gerard's in the clear, it's all down to Emmerich. I hope to hell he's still at the station, he's the one we want for all this."

"I've just spoken to Kenny, the mad professor's been charged with the lot and Kenny reckons that he has a lovely cast iron, high profile case to end his career." Came Paul's reply. "I'm on my way up."

Jordanna moved to Steve and tried to reason with him.

"Let us go? You've got Emmerich banged to rights, if you allow us time to leave, we will never return to Mortal Dean. What do you think Mr Speed, do you have as kind a soul as Gerard has?"

Steve thought for a second and then said.

"It doesn't excuse you for what you've done to Rita, she'll be scarred for life."

"I am sorry that she got caught up in all this, but we all carry our scars with us, if I had any choice at that time, I would never have gone there and hurt her," said Gerard.

Steve nodded and understood where Gerard was coming from.

"If I do let you go, promise me that I will never see you two again?" Insisted Steve.

"When Rita recovers, should you need money for skin grafts, I will help," offered Jordanna.

They moved away to the wagon waiting in the bay, Gerard just looked at Steve, not knowing what to do and then Steve came up with an idea.

"You should punch me or something, oh, and make it look good okay."

Steve angled his jaw so that Gerard had an area to target, and he planted a right hook to his temple and knocked the Detective out cold. Jordanna and Gerard ran off and met up with Gregg, they all got into the wagon and drove away out of the south exit.

Shabby was still sitting with Georgina, her company was pleasing and didn't want to leave her and he was still feeling protective towards her for what her father had done to her. He wanted her so much, nothing else mattered, he held her chin and gazed into her eyes, she looked back in his. She kissed him first and they stayed like that for a while just kissing.

Kenny had a pleased look on his face and at last he had the case sewn up. He thought he should thank Steve and Paul when they returned to the Station, as time was ticking on; he needed to know Steve was safe and well. Back at the factory Paul had found Steve sprawled out on the loading bay floor, he tapped his face lightly and Steve roused from his black out.

"He must have knocked me out, and gone out that way," Steve said, lying through his teeth.

"Is he still angry? He might kill again, how did he get the jump on you?" Asked Paul.

Steve shrugged and explained,

"When you counted to ten loudly, he somehow became normal,"

"But he is still at large, we must find him," insisted Paul.

"Look I don't think he will kill anybody else, all the people that harmed him are dead, there's nobody else," replied Steve.

"Well at least you're alright," said Paul grudgingly, agreeing with him.

"He didn't want to kill me, just to explain why he did it and now we know that his father, Emmerich made him do it all, without his knowledge or collaboration," added Steve.

"Let's get you back to the station, you'll have a lovely shiner in the morning," said Paul. "Where would Gerard go anyway?" He continued.

"Well if I were him, I would visit Michaela, to make sure that counting doesn't bring the nasty side of me out again," reasoned Steve.

They reached Steve's car and Paul took off the handcuffs, he rubbed his wrists and relished his freedom. He started his car and headed back to the station, on the way over he was thinking about his career, he'd spent twenty-five years in CID, nothing on this scale had ever happened to him before. He was glad that Emmerich would be put away for the rest of his life and kept away from Gerard, he was a bit disappointed to let him go, but the man did make a point about the scars people carry. He secretly hoped that Gerard would find peace with himself, knowing what he'd done to those people; it could break a person completely. After being used terribly by the people he counted on the most, Steve knew that Michaela was the only person who could help Gerard with that. He wouldn't want that nightmare hanging over him, and continued his drive to the station.

Gregg had driven Jordanna and Gerard out of Mortal Dean, and pulled his huge wagon up outside Michaela's house. Gerard hugged his brother and got out, helped Jordanna down and then spoke to Gregg.

"Listen, tell Mother and Georgie I'll be in touch, soon as things settle down, you're the man now so take care of them both."

Gregg nodded and drove away. Gerard and Jordanna walked up the driveway of Michaela's and rang the gong. Franks answered and breathed a sigh of relief.

"Thank goodness, you're safe, it has just come on the news that the Professor has been charged with all eleven murders and will probably spend the rest of his life behind bars," revealed Franks.

Gerard embraced his old friend and they went inside to see Michaela, who was watching the news on the television, as she turned to look at Gerard there was no emotion at all, she stood and hugged Jordanna, then walked with Gerard to her office.

"Well Emmerich can't harm anyone else with his mind games anymore, who wants a drink?" Michaela asked. Jordanna accepted but Gerard declined, he wanted something else from the Doctor.

"I want your help by getting Emmerich's message out of me, so that I can never go off like that again," he pleaded.

She nodded and laid him back on the couch, then asked Franks to take Jordanna out with him and make her feel comfortable. Again, she warmed his forehead and Gerard began to relax and as she counted down from ten, her hypnosis worked as usual, this time she spoke confidently and said.

"When I count back up to ten, you will no longer be pre-conditioned to hypnosis, Emmerich will not be able to control you again, one, two, three, four, five, six, seven, eight, nine, ten, awaken." Gerard came to and felt completely at ease with himself.

"Now take that wonderful girl with you and enjoy your lives," said Michaela. Gerard thanked Michaela and left with Jordanna. With her fortune, they'd live like royals.

Steve arrived back at the station weary, but enlightened, as he walked through he was met with a wall of officers, they crowded him out and began slapping him on the back.

"Kenny, can I have a word in your office?" Steve asked and they walked away from the huddle of colleagues; as they approached Kenny's office, Simon was coming along the corridor with Emmerich and Darren, they stopped as he approached.

"What you did to that boy was far worse than his tormentors did, for a father hurting their children is the worst thing a parent can do, I hope you can live with yourself," snapped Steve, right in the face of Emmerich while he said it.

"Take the prisoner away from here, Darren? Before there are blows thrown," ordered Kenny.

The remand officers took Emmerich away, and the station went quiet again. As Kenny and Steve came to the office, the door opened, Shabby and Georgina came out, and their clothing looked untucked. Kenny had his hands on his hips, he was looking at Shabby, Georgina was looking at Kenny and Steve was staring at Georgina.

"Good result Steve, well done," said Shabby and moved past him.

"You, sly dog," said Steve, on the way past.

Shabby walked away with Georgina, his arm was around her waist, and her hand in the back pocket of Shabby's trousers. Steve was relieved they'd finally got together, but Kenny wasn't very amused.

"Next time use your own damn office, not mine," he chipped in.

Steve and Kenny went into the now vacant office and Kenny headed straight for the whiskey.

"Shabby is right, you did well tonight, here have a drink with me, this is your best case and we've solved it together, just like the old times," said Kenny.

Steve reached into his pocket and took out his warrant card; he stared hard at it, took the poured whiskey from Kenny and downed it in one go.

"Thanks for your faith in me Guv, but I think it's a little late for back slaps, Gerard still got away. So as of today, I resign from the force, to focus of getting Rita better, thanks Kenny anyway." Kenny wasn't surprised by this, but was still sad to see a good Detective Constable go.

"Okay Steve, sorry to see you leave, you'll be a hard act to follow, who could fill your space?" Asked Kenny.

"Why don't you give Simon a go, I'll bet he'd make an excellent Detective, just needs someone to steer him right, but I reckon he won't let you down," replied Steve.

Kenny stroked his chin and found the suggestion appealing. They shook hands and Steve went to say goodbye to his colleagues, starting with Paul and shook his hand and said.

"I reckon this will get you to Inspector, if it doesn't, I want that fifty pound back."

Paul laughed and replied.

"Fifty quid, you're on mate."

Paul knew he would see Steve around they were good friends. Lana came over next and hugged Steve; she beamed at him and said.

"Looks like Brenda has you all to herself now, lucky cow."

Steve finally went to Shabby, Georgina and Simon who were waiting, after finding out his bombshell.

"Well this looks like one case that I've solved without you, mate," said Steve smiling at Shabby.

"Well when you've got something this beautiful holding you up, you mustn't disappoint her," joked Shabby as they shook hands, Steve then kissed Georgina and said very quietly.

"Gerard is safe, he will probably be in touch soon, just give him time to sort out some problems," he reassured her. She looked pleased and realized that Steve could have caught him, but let him escape.

"And finally, Detective Constable Simon Hixson, you've worked hard for this, so be grateful, try not to let them ride you too much, be your own man," Steve insisted.

"Thanks for putting in a good word for me Steve, have a quiet retirement, and good luck mate," replied Simon.

With all the farewells finished, Steve left the station for the last time, as he turned and looked back, he reflected on the last three weeks. He got to his car, started it, and drove to be with Brenda and Rita at the hospital.

Emmerich Deichmann had a quick appearance before the magistrates the following Friday morning and was remanded in custody while the prosecution prepared its case. Basil Granger applied for bail but the police objected, so Emmerich was taken to prison, still secretly hoping he would be acquitted. However, it appeared Gerard was nowhere to be seen, despite Emmerich's protests that he was the perpetrator. All the witnesses were watertight, Shabby's evidence, both Steve and Saul's testimony and Gerard's conversations with Michaela, all stacked up against Emmerich. He had no chance of getting off and even fired Basil for his incompetence. If the twelve good men and ladies of the jury find Emmerich guilty and because manipulating a man to commit murder under the state of hypnosis is classed as premeditated murder, the Judge could give him eleven life sentences. He was driven to the prison, the date set for his trial on the 19th December. Emmerich was stripped, his clothing and effects put in a box; then he had to have a bath before given his prison blue shirt, grey trousers and slip on shoes. The prison officers escorted him down D Wing and into a cell on his left.

"In you go Prof.," said the guard.

Emmerich stepped in, and lying on the right-hand bunk was another man, he had no hair, heavy beard and looked about sixty, he was shorter and he stank of body odour. This made Emmerich wince, as he breathed it in.

"Well, say hello to your new cellmate Barker, you'll be spending a bit of time together," said the other guard as they locked the cell door and left the two men alone getting acclimatized to one another.

To which the other cellmate just replied. "I hope you don't play chess pal, I fucking don't." He rolled over on to his side and ignored him.

❖

THE END

You Reap What You Sow!

Is dedicated to Mr Dean Workman. A Fantastic Human Being. You will be pleased with how the story turned out.

The input for some of the ideas are yours, so I must give you credit for that, otherwise the story could not have been written.

Sadly you're not here for me to hand a copy over.

But you will be proud to know that I kept my promise.

And given a copy to Tyrese. Thanks Dean!

Your good Butty, Nat (Reed Lovac)

Mortal Dean forever!

LOOK OUT FOR:

BOOK II
A WINTER HARVEST

COMING SOON